For my wonderful editors, Stephanie and Alice.
SERENA

For Anisha superfan, Poppy. And for Dylbo Baggins –
forever my Milo inspiration.
EMMA

First published in the UK in 2022 by Usborne Publishing Ltd., Usborne House,
83-85 Saffron Hill, London EC1N 8RT, England, usborne.com

Usborne Verlag, Usborne Publishing Ltd., Prüfeninger Str. 20,
93049 Regensburg, Deutschland VK Nr. 17560

ANISHA
ACCIDENTAL DETECTIVE

HOLIDAY ADVENTURE!

SERENA PATEL
Illustrated by Emma McCann

USBORNE

CHAPTER ONE

INTO THE FOREST WE GO!

The worst thing has happened. I mean, maybe not the worst, but it's pretty bad.

We're going on a **HOLIDAY ADVENTURE!** A holiday **with** adventure in it. I don't know if you've noticed, but I'm not exactly the adventurous type. I mean, I don't mind a bit of walking when it's sunny, and staying by a lake (which we are, apparently) could be kind of pretty, but **adventure** suggests climbing, swimming, attaching myself to harnesses and swinging about from a height. **NO**. That is not my idea of fun. Being terrified is not fun.

In fact, it could actually be my worst nightmare,

the worst type of holiday I could think of.

Of course, I'm the only person in my family who thinks this holiday adventure is a bad idea. Everyone else is super excited!

"Did you know there are hundreds of native species of wildlife in Sherwood Forest?" was the first thing my best friend Milo asked me when Mum and Dad announced we were going on a family break to the home of Robin Hood, and that Milo could come too.

My cousin Manny had replied, "Did **YOU** know the forest can be an **extremely** dangerous place! Luckily, I know all the top survival tips and I can build us a shelter out of twigs and leaves! I've been watching this documentary with one of the UK's top survivalists and he says we can learn to be at one with nature. He teaches something called '**bushcraft**', which is all about living off the forest and using things around you to survive. I'm learning everything I can about it. It could save your life one day!"

"Umm, I think we're going to be staying in a perfectly safe lodge, Manny, but it's good to know we'll be alright if we do run into trouble," Dad had chuckled.

That was two weeks ago and Milo has been researching all those hundreds of species ever since. He's got a fact file and everything! Manny, in the meantime, started packing his essential survival kit straight away, including a funnel for catching rainwater and a first-aid kit for the injuries he imagines we will all be getting. He's even convinced his dad to buy a set of four walkie-talkie radios for us to use. According to Manny, you can't rely on Wi-Fi in the forest so we need an emergency mode of communication. I've tried not to worry about what emergencies might happen and instead think of things I might be able to do while the others are swinging about on ropes or whatever.

Now we're all packed into the minibus Dad borrowed for the trip and finally driving down the longest, most winding, tree-lined path I've ever seen.

"There are more trees than I imagined," Mum remarks.

"It's the forest, dear, it's kind of expected that there will be trees," Dad answers.

"We grew up climbing trees," Granny says.

We all turn to look at her, except Dad, who is driving.

"Granny, you climbed trees?" I ask, not able to imagine it at all.

Granny smiles. "I wasn't always your granny, **beta**. I was a young girl once. I did all kinds of adventurous things – much to the despair of your great-grandmother, my mum, who just wanted me to be calm and quiet."

"Hmm," says Dad. "I kind of wish you would be a bit calmer now, Mum!"

We all laugh then, because my Granny Jas is not your average granny at all and totally not very calm or quiet either.

Just then we see the sign for the car park and we enter a clearing. There are lots of people milling around, some on bikes. Dad carefully drives round

and finds a space. Thankfully his parking skills have improved since the last time we took a family trip in this huge minibus!

We all pile out and look around. Directly in front of us is a building with a big sign that says **RECEPTION**. Just to the side of the double glass doors is the most **unexpected** thing! A giant white duck sculpture! It's about as tall and wide as a doorway. It has big wings made of strips of fabric that look like feathers. It's very grand and I notice

it's wearing a necklace that says **Delilah**.

"Wow, that is a big duck." Mindy whistles.

"I think it's cute!" says Milo.

"Of course you do," Manny grins. "I'm not sure your mum will let you bring that one home though!"

"I'm going to find some real ducks! I read they have whole families of ducks that nest here every year!" Milo replies happily.

"I've never made a duck curry." Granny grins mischievously.

Milo looks horrified. "You wouldn't, would you, Granny?"

Granny smiles. "No, **beta**, I wouldn't. I'm just messing with you."

Mindy cackles. "Granny's got jokes!"

Milo sniffs. "Protecting our wildlife is no joke!"

Granny looks worried then. "Oh, **beta**, I really was only joking. I didn't mean it."

Milo cracks up laughing. "I know, Granny – had you going there for a second though!"

Granny chuckles, relieved. "Phew, yes of course, I knew that!"

Mum, Dad, Aunty Bindi and Uncle Tony wander over from the minibus.

"What are you all giggling about? No time for that, we need to get checked in," Dad says. "I cannot wait to get back to nature."

"When were you in nature before?" Mum asks.

"Well, you know what I mean. They say being at one with nature is very good for the mind,"

Dad huffs. "I need all the stress relief I can get."

Aunty Bindi smiles. "You go for it! I've decided I'm going to sign up for the first class I like the sound of. We're going to do it **together**, aren't we, sweetums?" She turns adoringly to Uncle Tony.

"Umm, yeah, but not dancing, okay? You remember how our wedding dance went," he replies.

Aunty Bindi looks offended. "I thought our wedding dance was lovely. My friend Tina said I looked like that woman off Strictly! I think I'd be good on that show, you know," she says wistfully.

Just then another family walk past us, two grown-ups and a boy. The two adults go into the building, but the boy approaches us. "This place is awesome!" he says, holding out his hand. "I'm Dillon."

Dad goes to shake his hand, but as they touch there's a sharp buzzing sound and Dad yelps, pulling his hand back and shaking it in pain. It looks like the boy has a little electric buzzer in the palm of his hand and he's deliberately given Dad a shock!

Dillon rolls around laughing. "**Prank!**" he screams.

Dad frowns. "Yes, um, well, you'd better run along and follow your parents."

"That's okay. They won't even notice I'm not there and they'll be back out in a minute anyway." Dillon shrugs. "Hey, do you want to see something cool?"

Granny looks at him suspiciously. "I'm not sure, do we?"

"Oh, you definitely do," Dillon says confidently. "Look!" He holds out his other hand, which is closed in a fist.

Aunty Bindi steps forward. "What is it?"

Dillon grins. "Give me your hand."

"I don't think you should, Aunty Bindi," I say
warily.

"It's nothing bad," Dillon says.

So Aunty Bindi puts out her hand. Dillon places
his fist over her hand and drops something into it.

Aunty Bindi squeals. "**Eeeeeeeeeeeek!** Is that
a spider?!" She shakes her hand and the big, rather
furry thing in her hand goes flying. We all jump back
startled. It lands on Uncle Tony, who shrieks too and
jumps about a metre into the air.

Dillon howls, "**PRANK!!!!**
It's not real! **HAHA
HAHAHA!**"

Granny Jas steps forward as Aunty Bindi and Uncle Tony cling onto each other. "Now listen here, that is not very nice, is it?" she says sternly.

"Just a joke." Dillon shrugs.

"It's not very funny," I say.

Before he gets a chance to reply, Dillon's parents come back out and call him over. He sticks his tongue out at me and runs over to them. "Laters!" he calls out.

I hear his dad say, "Making friends?"

"Not really, they were a bit boring," Dillon replies.

"He was annoying!" I say.

"Yeah, really annoying," Mindy agrees.

"Don't worry," I say. "It's a big forest, we probably won't see him again!"

FOREST OF ADVENTURE

CHAPTER TWO

THE FUN BEGINS!

"Right," says Dad, "let's get checked in and get the keys to our lodge. You all wait here."

He and Mum are about to go inside but we're interrupted by a loud cheery voice. "Welcome, family, welcome to the **Forest of Adventure Holiday Park**!"

We all look over to where the voice came from. Approaching us is a tall muscular man, wearing a polo shirt and combat trousers.

Dad reaches out to shake his hand. "I'm Mr Mistry and this is my family," he says.

The man beams at us. "I'm Mr Gilbert – call me Tom. I'm the manager and owner of the park."

Granny eyes him up and down. "You're a bit young to own a park, aren't you, **beta**?"

Dad nudges her. "Mum!"

Tom laughs. "No offence taken. This park has been in my family for three generations. My grandfather only recently retired and put me in charge, so I have big footsteps to follow in!"

Aunty Bindi leaps forward. "I'm Bindi and this is my husband Tony. We're so excited to be here. I saw on your website that you run lots of classes and activities, and I want to try **everything**!" she says enthusiastically.

Tom beams. "I'm very glad to hear it. I'll grab you an activity schedule, but firstly let me invite you all to a gathering we are having in the main square today. It starts in a minute, actually, and it's a get-to-know-you barbecue!"

Manny's ears prick up. "Will there be food?"

"Plenty of it!" Tom nods.

"We're there," Milo says. "Count us in!"

"I've got a question," I say.

"Of course, that's what I'm here for!" Tom says.

"The big duck, what's that all about?"

Tom's eyes light up. "Well, Delilah is a part of our forest family here. Years ago, when the park first opened and there was still some construction going on, my grandfather rescued a family of ducks and guided them to the safety of the lake.

The mother duck came back year after year and my grandfather was very fond of her. He named her Delilah and decided she should be the park mascot. Of course, the real Delilah wasn't quite so big!" he jokes. "Actually, Delilah has been the mascot of the park ever since it opened, which is fifty years this year. We're planning a huge celebration in a couple of days, so if you're here for three nights you'll be able to come along. We had the big sculpture made specially to mark the occasion! It was quite a project and all the team who work here helped. The anniversary is going to be a really special day, because we're going to surprise my grandfather and bring him here to see all the festivities. We've been planning it for weeks!"

"Sounds fun. You know, I'm a bit of an expert party planner," Aunty Bindi says. "I could help if you need it."

Tom smiles. "I think we've got it in hand, thank you. Anyway, you're on your holidays, let us look after you!"

"We just need to check in, I think," says Dad.

"This way then!" Tom says, leading Mum and Dad into the main building in front of us. The rest of us wait outside with Granny, Uncle Tony and Aunty Bindi.

"I'm so excited!" squeals Bindi.

"You know, I think I might try a new activity too," Granny Jas says. "Never too old to learn."

"I can teach you some survival skills," says Manny. "I borrowed a great book from the library. It's called **One Hundred Ways To Stay Alive In The Jungle!**"

Granny raises an eyebrow. "We're not in the jungle, **beta**, and I think I will be okay – I've survived this long!"

Manny frowns. "There are lots of hidden dangers, Granny. For example, did you know that eating the leaves of the foxglove plant can cause poisoning?"

Granny laughs. "I won't eat any flowers, don't worry, **beta**. But that is useful to know, thank you."

Manny huffs. "You'll all be wanting my help soon, just watch. Out here in the **wilderness** anything can happen!" He gestures around him excitedly.

Mindy snorts. "Don't be so dramatic! Anyway, remember when we went camping with Dad that time? You made us come home early because you were scared of the noises in the field."

Manny grunts. "Yeah, well cows can be quite **aggressive**, you know."

Milo interrupts. "I know an interesting fact about cows. They bring up their partly digested food and chew on it for up to eight hours a day."

"**EWWW**, Milo!" we all say.

Milo shrugs. "It stopped you arguing."

And then we all laugh because he's right as usual.

A few seconds later Mum and Dad come back out. They're not alone though. Walking with them is a girl, probably about sixteen or seventeen years old, and she's wearing a green and white park uniform.

"Hi," she says, "I'm Cleo. Tom asked me to show you all to the barbecue."

We all introduce ourselves and then follow Cleo as she walks us round the park towards the main square.

"So, what are you looking forward to most? We have some great activities here," she says.

"Umm, I'm not really an 'activities' type of person," I say. "I kind of feel like I'm on the wrong holiday, to be honest," I whisper to her.

Cleo smiles. "I used to feel a bit like that too. But I've realized through working here that you haven't got to be running around the whole time to enjoy being in the forest." She waves at a girl walking past wearing the same uniform as her. "I'll drop your jumper off later!" she shouts.

She turns back to me. "Sorry, that's my friend, Rae – we swap clothes all the time. I keep forgetting to give her back her jumper. Anyway, where was I? Oh yeah, there's some really nice walks here – and we have a reading nook."

My ears prick up. "A reading nook?"

"Yep, it's really cool. I go there sometimes on my break."

I smile now too. Maybe there will be something on this holiday for me!

CHAPTER THREE

DANGER EVERYWHERE!

"Are we there yet? My feet hurt!" Aunty Bindi groans as we turn another corner.

"Stop moaning! When we were children in India,* we walked miles to school every day. Miles, I tell you! In no shoes!" Granny says.

"We'll be there in a minute, I'm sure," says Dad, looking uncertain.

"We can look out for wildlife on the way," Milo suggests.

"Or **danger!**" says Manny, narrowing his eyes and looking around.

* Granny Jas grew up in Mumbai, India. I've never been but Granny says it was an amazing place to live and she wants us all to go there on a holiday. I'm not sure about ALL OF US together on a plane for eight hours!

"The only danger is of you getting left here for being so annoying!" mutters Mindy.

"Children!" Mum warns.

Cleo interrupts. "We're not far now, don't worry."

As we walk a little further I can already hear laughter and music – and the smell of the barbecue is **amazing**. A few moments later we walk around the corner to see the square Tom had mentioned.

We step through a rainbow-coloured balloon arch and are immediately welcomed by a stilt walker!

Cleo nods at him. "Jamil, this is the Mistry family. Tom asked me to make sure they got here okay and this is their first time in the forest, so we want to make sure they have an awesome time!"

"Hello!" Jamil says, bending down. "I'm Jamil. Help yourselves to food and drink. There's lots of activities over in the tent too, for children **AND** grown-ups." He grins.

Aunty Bindi squeals, "**Yay!** Let's go and see!" and drags Uncle Tony away towards the little green tent.

There are lots of families here. There are little kids running around, yelling and laughing, grandparents trying to chase after them and parents, uncles, aunties and friends chatting, eating and smiling.

"Shall we get some food?" Dad asks.

"**YES PLEASE!**" Manny and Milo shout together.

So we join the line for the buffet. I'm actually quite hungry now, and we all pile our plates high with salad, corn on the cob, chicken, bread and coleslaw. **Yum yum!**

"Where shall we sit?" I ask, looking around.

"There are some spots right over here on the grass," Cleo says.

We plonk ourselves down with our plates and drinks.

"Which are the best activities you have here?" Mindy asks.

"Ooh, all sorts!" Cleo answers. "Dancing, singing, baking, drawing, painting, archery, indoor rock climbing, nature walks, horse riding – there's even a zip wire."

Granny rubs her chin. "Archery, you say. I might give that a try."

Dad frowns. "The bow might be a bit heavy, Mum, and the arrows might be a bit sharp."

Granny waves him away like she always does. "Will you stop fussing! Are you **MY** mother?"

Dad goes pink. "No, Mum."

I smile. Granny Jas never takes no for an answer once she decides she wants to do something. So she **WILL** be trying archery.

Mum turns to Dad. "We could try the baking together. We haven't done anything just us two for ages. You used to make amazing brownies, remember?"

Dad nods. "I was a bit of a **whizz** in the kitchen when I was younger, wasn't I?"

"What shall we do?" Mindy asks me. "Rock climbing sounds fun."

"I don't like heights much," I admit. "But you go ahead. Being here is a chance for everyone to do something they like."

"I want to meet the horses," says Milo. "I bet they have some interesting tales to tell."

"Yeah, swishy ones!" Manny jokes.

Just then Aunty Bindi and Uncle Tony come bounding over. Aunty Bindi has a butterfly painted on her face and Uncle Tony is a tiger!

"This place is **amazing!**" Aunty Bindi shrieks.
"We just signed up for an art class. And did you
know there's entertainment every evening, and
a disco?"

Uncle Tony looks less excited. "I'm not sure
about the art class, sweetums. I never was very good
at drawing."

Aunty Bindi grins. "Then you'll be super happy,

because when you went to the loo I volunteered you to be the life model for the class to draw."

Uncle Tony looks horrified. Mindy and Manny stifle giggles and Milo just says, "Cool!"

"Life model? Aren't they usually, like, you know, not wearing clothes?" Dad asks warily.

"Well, usually, yes, but we thought it would be fun if Tony dressed up in a toga, like a Roman!" Bindi squeals, clearly very pleased with her idea.

Uncle Tony looks a bit green now. "I think I need some air," he says, walking away.

"But we're already outside!" Aunty Bindi runs after him, but keeps stopping every few seconds to compliment someone on their outfit or hair.

I look at Cleo. "I'd like to say our family is not always like this but that's not true." I sigh.

Cleo laughs. "You should meet my family! You know my nan once sent an email to my boss at my last job to tell him off for not giving me a pay rise! So **embarrassing!**"

"Oh wow," I say. "My Granny Jas is always saying she'll come down to school to sort people out, but thankfully she hasn't done it yet."

"So, do you want to see the reading nook, Anisha?" Cleo asks me.

"Ooh, yes please!" I say.

So while the others look at the activities schedule and start picking what they want to do for the next few days, Cleo and I take a walk.

"Family trips are pretty **full-on**, huh?" Cleo asks me.

"Yeah, and my family are full-on even on a normal day at home." I sigh. "I'm just not into the things they're into. It's hard sometimes being the odd one out!"

"Ah, it's okay to be into different things, Anisha. I think it's good to be different! Take me, for example – I'm totally different to my older brother. He's into weird rock music and films that have subtitles, while I'm into space and science."

I stop walking. "Are you kidding? **I'm** into space and science!" I exclaim.

"No way!" Cleo beams. "That's so cool."

"Which is your favourite planet?" I ask.

Cleo grins, and we say it at the same time:

"**Venus!**"

"I wish they'd do more voyages to Venus, but everyone is all about Mars," she complains.

"I know, so annoying!" I laugh.

As we walk along I realize the **knot** in my stomach has loosened. I'm starting to feel more relaxed – it's just so nice to talk to someone on my wavelength. We soon come to a clearing and Cleo stands in front of me.

"Are you ready?" she asks.

I nod. "I think so."

Cleo steps aside and suddenly I'm looking at the most **gorgeous** reading nook I've ever seen. There's a wooden covered bench with two comfy looking chairs in front of it and a bookcase to the side, filled

with books. Hanging from the trees are coloured ribbons and lights.

"It's so pretty," I whisper.

"And calm!" says Cleo. "It's one of my favourite places in the park."

"I **love** it. I can't wait to bring a blanket and a flask of hot chocolate down here with my book," I say.

"Sounds perfect," says Cleo.

Just then we hear a twig cracking.

"Is someone there?" Cleo calls out.

Silence.

"Probably just a bird or something," she reassures me. But then, as we're about to start chatting again, there's a loud "**BOO!**" and someone jumps out from behind a tree at us! Oh, it's that boy from earlier, Dillon. It startles us both and we grab each other.

Dillon cracks up laughing. "**HAAAAAAAAAA! GOTCHA!**" he shouts.

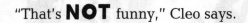

"That's **NOT** funny," Cleo says.

"Lurking behind trees and scaring people is not the kind of behaviour we expect here. It's a **RELAXING** place."

Dillon just shrugs. "**WHATEVER**, just trying to have a laugh – this place is so boring." And he runs off!

"That boy is **rude**!" Cleo says.

"I know, he already pranked us twice. I'm hoping we can just steer clear of him for the rest of the weekend, but I feel like he's going to pop up wherever we go," I say.

"Well, just come and tell me if he bothers you, we can have a word with his parents," Cleo says.

"Thanks," I say. "Have you worked here long?"

"It's my first summer here, actually. I'm working to save up some money to go to a special space camp in the autumn. It's a thing I found out about through sixth form. You get to go for two weeks and learn all about working in the industry. Places are limited though and it's **SO** expensive, so that's why I'm working this summer. It could be a real opportunity to meet people who have done what I want to do and I'm so **excited** about it!"

"Wow, sounds **cool**. I'd love to do something like that when I'm older," I say, impressed.

We start walking back, chatting all the way. We agree to meet up at some point tomorrow for some more book chat and hot chocolate. I'm starting to actually feel excited about this break!

"Hey, Neesh, how was the reading nook?" Milo asks when we get back to the main square.

"It was so cool!" I say.

A boy comes over then. He's about the same age as Cleo, maybe sixteen, and wearing the same shirt as her – green and white – and the jacket worn by everyone on the activities team, so he must work here as well.

"Hey, Cleo, Tom wants to see you," he says.

"Oh, okay, I'm coming. By the way, Bobby, this is the Mistry family. Make sure you look after them over the next few days, okay?"

Bobby just nods at us and then walks away.

Cleo smiles. "Don't mind him, he's always in a mood. Probably got told off for pulling another one of his silly pranks. He never learns!"

"**Ugh** he'd probably get on with that Dillon then!"

"Tom doesn't seem that strict," Milo says. "We met him earlier, he was really nice."

"You're a guest and he's not your boss! Plus, this fifty-years-of-the-park celebration has really got everyone stressed out. We want it to be perfect for Mr Gilbert Senior. He's really **lovely** and the park wouldn't be here if it weren't for him," Cleo tells us.

"The Delilah statue *is* amazing," Milo says.

"Thank you. She took ages to make, but I think Mr Gilbert Senior is going to love her! Anyway, I'd better go. Don't forget to sign up for all those fab activities and I'll see you later," Cleo says as she heads off.

"She was nice," says Mindy. "This break is going to be fun."

"Ooh, they've brought cakes out. Let's grab some," Mum suggests.

As I'm about to follow her to the buffet table, I hear some **shrieks** and notice that boy Dillon is over there, pranking some kids. He's using his pretend spider again. He just doesn't stop.

Granny Jas notices him too. "That boy is a show-off," she mutters.

"Yeah, he's super annoying," I agree.

"Well, don't let him spoil your time here, **beta**. Looks like you made a nice friend with that girl, Cleo."

"I really did, she's so nice, Granny. Maybe this weekend won't be a **total** disaster after all," I say.

CHAPTER FOUR

DISORIENTED DUCKS!

The rest of the barbecue is fun – Mindy and I share the biggest slice of rainbow cake I've ever seen, and it's so delicious! We see the park staff bustling about and chatting to guests. I notice that grumpy boy Bobby painting pottery with some children, and he looks less grumpy now.

We look at the map of the park and it's so big! I'm still not keen on trying any of the scary activities but now I've seen the reading nook and met Cleo, I feel like this holiday could still be fun for me after all.

After a while the barbecue gets quieter and most people start leaving. It's mainly just the staff tidying up by the time we get up to go.

"Right, family, let's go and find our lodge," Dad says, holding up a key.

"I'm excited to see where we're sleeping," Mum says.

"Bagsy the best room!" shouts Manny as we walk along the path.

"See you later, Delilah," says Milo, tipping his cap to the big duck sculpture as we go past her, and then we all pile back in the minibus to drive round to our lodge.

Our lodge is number 452 and it's right at the other end of the park. Dad drives slowly along the windy forest paths and eventually pulls up outside it. It's a two-storey, five-bedroom lodge and it looks like a proper little forest house with walls made of huge logs – it's awesome! We're all so excited that we pile out of the minibus for the second time at super speed. Mindy grabs the key from Dad and we leave the grown-ups to unload all the luggage while we run to the front door and let ourselves in. We head straight into the living room, which has a big TV and a corner sofa. It's an open-plan layout, so the kitchen is right there for drinks and snacks. Mindy runs to the patio doors, which lead out into the forest.

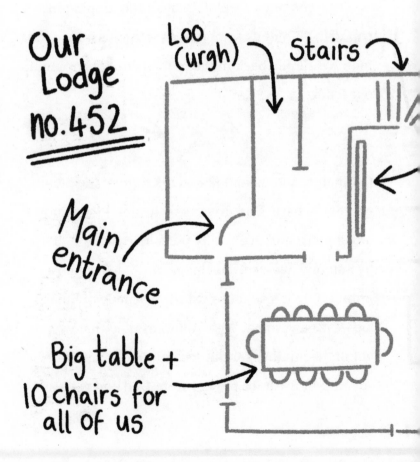

Our Lodge no.452

Loo (urgh)

Stairs

Main entrance

Big table + 10 chairs for all of us

"We've got our own little seating area here too!" she says, opening the doors.

"**Woah!**" Milo exclaims. "Can we just stay here for ever?"

"Let's go and see the bedrooms," Manny suggests.

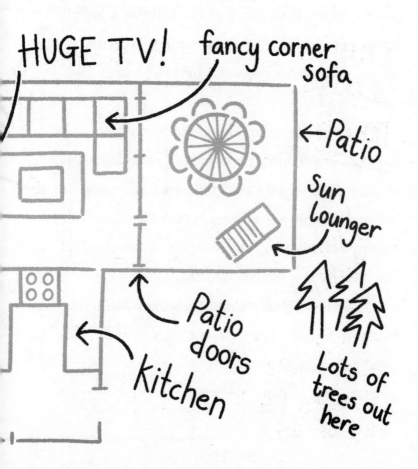

HUGE TV!

fancy corner sofa

←Patio

Sun lounger

Patio doors

Kitchen

Lots of trees out here

"I thought you wanted to get the real outdoors experience and camp outside?" Mindy teases.

"Well, you know, we are here for three nights. It wouldn't hurt to stay inside on one or two of those," Manny replies as we go upstairs.

At the top of the stairs is a landing and six doors, leading to one bathroom and five bedrooms. We all run in and out of the rooms, shouting, "This one's mine – oh, wait, that one's bigger! No, I want that one!"

We agree Mindy and I will share and Manny and Milo can share. Mindy and I take a room at the front of the lodge. It's got a skylight, which is awesome, because at night we'll be able to see the stars. Manny and Milo take the room opposite ours and I can hear them jumping on the beds already.

"Are you lot going to help us bring some of this stuff in?" Mum calls up. "You know some of it does belong to you too!"

"Coming!" we shout down.

Just as we're leaving our rooms, we hear an almighty screech.

"Aaaaaaaaaah!" It's Aunty Bindi.

Manny rushes off in front. "I bet it's a poisonous spider, or maybe a snake! I'll need my anti-venom kit," he says. "This could be **life or death!**"

"Wait, what? Where did you even—" Mindy starts as we follow him down the stairs.

But when we reach the living room, we see it's not a spider or a snake that has made Aunty Bindi screech and jump into Uncle Tony's arms.

"Oh, they're just ducks!" says Milo. "Look, they're a family!" he says, pointing at the three little brown-and-yellow ducklings trailing behind the larger adult duck, who is also brown with a bright blue patch on her wing. I guess she's the mum.

"Yeah, there are ducks **INSIDE** the **HOUSE!**" Bindi squeals.

"What are they doing in here?" Dad asks and then he looks at the patio doors. "Ah, I see, someone

left them open and they've wandered in. We just
need to guide them back out again."

"I'll help!" says Milo, our resident animal expert.

"Me too!" Manny adds.

"Ducks can be very protective of their babies."
Milo speaks softly. "Judging by the colour on the
mum's wing I think they're mallards. They're
probably just a bit lost. We have to be very **gentle**
and approach slowly. Move anything that's in the
way and we'll guide them back out through the patio
doors."

"I think I'll stay outside then," says Mum.

"And me!" says Aunty Bindi, jumping down and
running out the front door, dragging Uncle Tony
with her and almost knocking over Granny Jas.

"What is going on?" Granny asks. "Oh, ducks, of
course, why not?" She shakes her head, laughing.

"It's not funny, Mum!" Dad whispers. "We have
to get them out."

"That's easy!" Granny says, moving quickly
forward. "You just have to shoo them like this!"
And she grabs her sari and uses it like a sail to steer
the ducks. The mother duck doesn't like this though
and starts quacking, hissing and flapping her wings.
The baby ducks get all confused and make a shrill
whistling noise.

"I don't think they like that, Granny!" Milo says.

"Granny, why don't you go
outside and see if there
are any more bags to
bring in?"
I suggest.
"**Humph**. I
was trying to help!"
Granny huffs but
does as I've asked
and goes outside.

51

Aunty Bindi pops her head round the door. "Have they gone yet?"

"NO!" we all whisper-shout. The ducks are now flapping round in a circle and moving further away from the doors!

"Right, that's not working. We need a new tactic. I read somewhere that ducks find music calming," Milo says.

"I'll play some on my phone," Manny says.

"What about treats? What do ducks eat?" Mindy asks.

"Slugs and snails," Milo replies.

"**EWW**, we are not bringing slugs and snails in here, Milo," I say. "What else?"

"Lettuce, cucumber and carrot might be good if we lay a little trail out of the lodge for them. Or some grains," Milo says.

"Okay, I'll see if we've got any of those things in the groceries bag Mum packed," I say. "You calm them down with some music."

I run outside, where Mum, Granny, Uncle Tony and Aunty Bindi are all sitting on the grass. "I thought you were unloading the minibus," I say.

"Where to? We can't take anything inside while the ducks are in there," Bindi moans, swatting imaginary flies from her face. "You didn't tell me there would be ducks!"

"Yeah, but you knew we were coming to the forest, Aunty. There's wildlife in the forest," I point out. "Mum, have we got any lettuce or cucumber or carrots in our groceries?"

"You want a snack, **beta**?" Mum asks.

"Not for me, for the ducks – to entice them out," I say.

"Ah, clever! Let's see what we've got."

Just as Mum's looking in the boxes, a car pulls up by our minibus. It must be the family staying in the next lodge. **Oh no!** As they step out of the car, I recognize the **annoying** boy from earlier, Dillon.

Mum waves at the parents. Dillon tries to get a

good look at what we're doing, but I grab the bits of food off Mum and run in. A nosy neighbour is all we need right now!

A few seconds later I'm back in the lodge, laying a trail of lettuce and some porridge oats. Manny has put on some classical music and is swaying at the front of the little duck line.

"Not like that! You have to **BE** a duck," Milo says. "Like this!"

Soon he and Manny are both **waddling** and **quacking** in front of the mummy duck, who looks totally unimpressed and sits down in the middle of the floor.

"Maybe the waddling is a bit distracting," I try to say, but no one is listening.

Dad sits down with his head in his hands. He's given up too!

"The poor ducklings look frightened," Mindy says. "**Shush**, you two!"

Finally, the boys stop and it's quiet. Then, just like that, Mummy duck gets up, quacks at her ducklings as if to say, *Come on then, little ones*, and, grabbing a bit of lettuce in her beak, she leads them out through the patio doors.

"Phew, thank goodness for that!" says Dad. "I'll go and let the others know it's safe to come in."

"Wow, we've only been here five minutes and we've already had a duck invasion," Manny says.

"Hardly an invasion," I point out. "I think they were just a bit disoriented."

"Yeah, but it still proves my point. Now seems like a good time to hand out the walkie-talkies actually. Here, keep one on you always and use in an emergency. We need to be on the lookout for danger at **ALL** times in **ALL** places," Manny says firmly.

"Duck danger?" Mindy chuckles.

"Ducks are lovely," says Milo dreamily.

"Let's put our stuff in our rooms," I say, as Dad plonks my pile of books in my arms.

We head upstairs together and Mindy and I start unpacking our things. I place my pile of books carefully on my bedside table, ready to dive into later.

"Are you planning to read all of those while we're here?" Mindy asks.

"Yep," I say happily. "I can't think of anything better."

"You do **realize** you're on holiday with all of us? So, the likelihood of everything going to plan is **zero,** right?" Mindy smiles.

"We're in the middle of nowhere. What could possibly happen here?" I say.

"Ha, you should know better than to ask that question, Anisha!" Mindy laughs.

CHAPTER FIVE

DUCK DISASTER!

The next morning, Dad announces we are going for a special treat – pancakes for breakfast at the park restaurant. Everyone is **very** excited.

"I'm having everything on mine," Milo declares.

"I just need a huge dollop of chocolate sauce on mine," says Mindy, licking her lips.

"I could have made pancakes here!" Granny Jas moans.

"Well, you're always looking after us all. I thought it would be nice for you to have someone bring you breakfast for a change," says Dad, putting an arm round Granny. "We'd better go, I booked for 8.30 and it's a little bit of a walk."

"That's zero-eight-thirty hours in military time, Uncle," Manny corrects him. "Now, before we leave, has everyone got their walkie-talkies?" he asks, dead seriously.

"No, but are you sure we need them?" I ask. "There's people everywhere and I don't think any of us are going to get that lost anyway."

Manny scoffs. "How naïve you are, Anisha. There is danger all around us! The radio is there for your safety," he replies sagely.

Uncle Tony pats him on the head. "All a bit serious for a Saturday morning, son. We'll take the walkie-talkies, okay? Do we need a code word?" he jokes.

Manny frowns at him. "Actually, yes. If you find yourself in trouble you need to say '**SOS!**' which means—"

"Save our socks?" Milo asks.

Manny sighs.

"Save our sandwiches?" Milo tries again.

"I know, I know – save our samosas!" Mindy jokes.

Manny rolls his eyes. "No, you know very well what it stands for, Mindy, because I already told you. It's '**Save our souls**'!"

"What does that mean? Sounds a bit scary to me. Why would our souls need saving?" Milo asks.

"It's an old saying. It just means you're in trouble and need help," Dad explains. "I think we all know what to do, Manny, thank you for sorting this out. I feel very safe now. Right, shall we go and get those pancakes?"

We walk to the restaurant with Manny directing everyone using the map app on his phone, and also looking through binoculars, for some reason. He gives us regular time checks too, in military time, of course. Very quickly it becomes **zero-eight-twenty** and we only have ten minutes to get to breakfast!

"Isn't this nice?" Aunty Bindi beams, linking arms with me. "We never walk anywhere any more.

We need to do it more often
and leave the cars at home.
Aren't there some hills near us?
We could totally walk up those
on a Sunday."

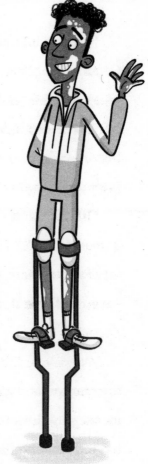

Just then, as we pass the
outdoor exercise equipment,
we see that stilt walker from the
barbecue yesterday – what was his
name? Jamil, that's it. I wonder if
he ever takes those stilts off! He
sees us and waves, but he looks a
bit nervous to me. Maybe he's shy.

"I'm gonna try stilt walking,"
Milo says. "It looks fun!"

"I'll give that one a miss," I mutter.

Soon we reach the restaurant and as we all go
past Delilah the duck sculpture, we give her a wave
and say good morning.

"She really is something," Mum remarks.

"All this fuss about a duck seems a little strange."
Granny Jas sniffs.

"Well, the celebration is for the park, Granny,
but Delilah is an important part of the park's
history," I say. "Like your community centre is
important to you."

Granny nods. "Ah, I see. Well, in any case I like
a good party."

"Right, where are those pancakes?" Dad says as
we enter the restaurant for breakfast right on time.

We emerge at 9.25 a.m. with full tummies and a plan
for the day. Everyone has activities they're going to
try and I'm planning to return to the reading nook.
But before any of us gets a chance to do anything,
we hear a **shriek** – and this time it's not coming
from Aunty Bindi.

It's coming from Delilah – or rather the woman
standing in front of her. But Delilah does not look

like herself at all. Delilah barely even looks like a duck any more! Poor Delilah is in **tatters!**

The woman standing there turns to face the small crowd that has now gathered. "I...I...I...found her like this. Who would do such a thing?" she stutters. I see from her badge and uniform that she works here. "I came out from the reception desk for my break and that's when I saw!" She points dramatically at Delilah.

We all stand in silence for a moment, trying to take in the sight before us. Poor Delilah the duck is a **mess**! She is missing one wing, which has left a ragged gaping hole, and she is covered in yellow gloop, as though someone has thrown a can of paint over her. There are splatters and splodges **everywhere**! I can't believe what I'm seeing.

"Delilah!" Milo cries out sadly.

"She was fine when we went past less than an hour ago," Mindy points out.

"Maybe it was foxes?" Manny suggests.

"Foxes couldn't throw paint all over her." Uncle Tony shakes his head. "Looks like vandalism to me."

I shiver. Could that be right? **Vandalism?** But why? And who?

I notice then that Tom the manager has arrived and is standing at the front in shock. Slowly he turns to the small team of staff standing at the side. "Did anyone see what happened?" he asks quietly.

Everyone shakes their heads, and I look closely for any reaction. They all look as confused as the rest of us.

Tom steps forward and examines the damage, his jaw clenched. "This looks deliberate. There would be no reason to have paint near Delilah and the wing has clearly been ripped off. You all know how important Delilah is to the park and to our family. **WE ARE** going to find out who did this and I feel sorry for them when we do."

As we're all standing there, trying to make sense of the sight in front of us, Cleo arrives with some of the entertainment team and steps forward. She looks so upset. "Mr Gilbert, how has this happened? I can't imagine anyone wanting to damage Delilah like this. And right before the celebration!"

Tom runs his fingers through his hair. "You're right, this is just the worst thing to happen before our big party. I don't know how we're going to get her clean and fixed up again in two days."

"We'll all help," Cleo says. "Won't we?" She looks at the team members behind her.

"**Nobody touch that duck!**" says a voice. We

look over and it's another man in a park uniform.
He has a beard and a moustache that twitches when
he talks.

"Excuse me, but don't we need to try and fix
her?" Cleo asks.

"Yes, but first I want to find out who caused this
damage!"

Milo nudges me. "Who do you think that is?"
he says, a bit too loudly.

The man looks over
at us and says, "I am
Mr Judge. I work
here as the
facilities
manager.
I make sure
everything runs
smoothly, and
when it does not,
I find out why!"

Tom speaks up then. "How shall we do this, Jim?" he asks Mr Judge.

"I'd like to examine the duck and then I'll need to question the staff," Mr Judge says, giving them a look that makes me **nervous** and I haven't even done anything wrong!

"Right, okay," says Tom. He turns to the guests, including our family. "I'm sorry your morning has been disrupted – please carry on and enjoy the rest of your day. We have this in hand now," he says, not convincingly at all.

I look at Cleo. "Can I stay here with Cleo?" I ask Mum. "We were going to spend some time at the reading nook together today, and I'm sure we can do that once she's spoken to Mr Judge. I'll catch you all up in a bit, I promise."

Mum frowns. "Shall I stay too?"

"No, you don't need to, Mum. Plus I have one of the walkie-talkies that Manny brought. I can radio you if there's a problem."

Mum sighs. "Okay. Right, everyone else, let's go. Grown-ups, we've all got activities starting in the next fifteen minutes – we'd better get a move on! I think Milo and Manny have something booked too? Mindy, you said you just want to explore a bit first?"

Mindy nods.

"**Hooray!** I'm off to see the horses?" Milo declares.

Manny says he's going to go off to join a nature-trail walk. "If we get lost, I can guide everyone back to safety using only my instincts," he says.

"And your compass app, plus the map in your pocket. Oh, and the guide will probably know where they're going too – that's kind of why they're the guide," Mindy says with a giggle.

"One day, you're going to be in **real trouble** and need my help and I might not feel like rescuing you!" Manny says, pulling a face.

"Oh yeah? Maybe I'll rescue myself!" Mindy retorts.

Finally, my family leave, but not before Manny tries to teach me how to tap out a Morse code **SOS** signal on the radio. "You never know when you'll need it," he says.

By the time I turn back to Delilah, Mr Judge is walking around her slowly, **umming** and **ahhing** to himself. Some chairs and a table have been placed nearby so that he and Tom can talk to each employee. A few staff go off to their duties, with a time to return in groups of five. Cleo is in the first group to be seen, so I stand with her in the short line while we wait for her turn.

"This is a nightmare," she murmurs. "I can't understand why anyone would do that."

"Don't worry," I say. "I'm sure they'll get to the bottom of it."

"Thanks for staying with me," Cleo says gratefully.

"That's okay," I say. "It's not a nice thing to face alone – plus, it got me out of having to be adventurous with my family." I grin.

We watch as each staff member gets grilled by Mr Judge. He seems to have a tactic of staring at everyone to make them as **uncomfortable** as possible. Then he scribbles notes furiously after they get up. A couple of the staff walk past us looking quite jittery after their chat with him.

Finally, it's Cleo's turn. She sits down and I stand behind her.

Mr Judge raises an eyebrow at me. "And you are?"

"She's a guest and a friend," Cleo answers. "We're going to the reading nook after this."

Tom nods. "It's fine."

Mr Judge clears his throat loudly. "Right, you're Cleo Constantine, is that correct?"

"Yes," Cleo answers calmly.

"You haven't worked here long, have you?" He scribbles something on the piece of paper he has in front of him.

"No, just a few weeks. But I love it here," Cleo replies.

"Hmm, well, can you tell me where you were at 8.30 this morning, please?"

Cleo looks panicked. "I...um...was in my room and I was getting ready for work. My first activity session isn't till 10 a.m. so I had a later start."

Mr Judge looks up. "Can anyone verify that?"

"Well, no, I have my own room. I was alone," Cleo explains.

"Aha, I see."

"Sorry, what do you mean?"

"You have no alibi." Mr Judge smirks.

"I don't understand...you can't think I did it!" Cleo protests.

"Well, **EVERYONE** is a suspect right now and I have to take **EVERYTHING** into account," Mr Judge says. "Now, tell me, how do you feel about Delilah? Do you hate her, hmm?" He narrows his eyes and stares at Cleo intently.

"**What? No!**" Cleo says. "Look, I'm sorry, but this is ridiculous. I didn't and would never damage any part of this park. You have to believe me!"

Tom smiles sympathetically at Cleo. "I know you wouldn't. Look, Jim, I think we're barking up the wrong tree here. Cleo isn't the one."

Mr Judge shrugs. "Just trying to get to the truth. Nothing personal."

Cleo looks annoyed. "Can I go now then?"

"Yes, that's fine. Thanks, Cleo," Tom answers.

Cleo goes to stand up, but as she does Mr Judge jumps up and grabs her arm.

"**Wait!**" he yells.

"What on earth…?

Let go of me!"

Cleo demands.

"**PAINT!**"

Mr Judge booms, pointing at the bottom of Cleo's park uniform jacket.

And that's when I see it too. **It can't be!** A bright yellow splodge of **paint** on the bottom of her jacket! It looks like a smudged handprint.

Cleo looks down, horrified. "No…I mean, I don't know how that got there! This isn't my normal jacket." She looks at me. "This is a big mistake!"

Tom stands up and walks round to examine Cleo's jacket. "Paint. Yellow paint. Just like on Delilah. No, it can't be. **Not you**, Cleo!" Tom says. "You wouldn't. Would you?"

Cleo cries, "No, of course not! I wouldn't. I couldn't! It's not what it looks like!" She tries to rub the stain desperately, then lifts her paint-smudged hands up to her face. "It wasn't me, I promise. I would never do such a thing!"

But it's no good. Tom goes quite red in the face – I'm worried he might explode. "No one else has paint on them, Cleo. You've got to admit, that's **VERY** incriminating. And you can't prove you were in your room. I don't know what I'm supposed to do here.

You're saying you didn't do it, but you have actual evidence on you that suggests otherwise."

"But it's not my jacket! When I was in the cafe this morning getting a drink, I managed to spill juice on myself, so I quickly threw my jacket in the laundry and grabbed a spare one off a hook in the staffroom. I figured it must belong to someone who isn't in today so it wouldn't matter. I never noticed the paint stain."

Mr Judge **scoffs**. "You expect us to believe that? The jacket clearly fits you perfectly!"

Tom looks at Mr Judge, who nods solemnly. He takes a deep breath. "I have no choice. I'm going to have to let you go, Cleo – you're **fired**. I can't believe you would let us all down like this." He shakes his head in disappointment.

I notice no one steps forward to defend Cleo. The few entertainment staff left in the line behind us look terrified, actually, and they seem to have stepped away from Cleo. She looks so small standing there by herself. I'm scared to speak up too, but I do it anyway.

I step forward. "Tom, I don't think that's right," I say. "Cleo wouldn't! I haven't known her very long but I'm **positive** she can't be the one who did that to Delilah! She's only working here so she can afford space camp. Why would she put that at risk?"

Tom turns to look at me. "Anisha, I appreciate you trying to help, but you've only been here five minutes. You're a guest – leave this to me and go and enjoy your break. Now, if you'll excuse me, I have to go and find someone who can fix our poor Delilah. Cleo, you've got the weekend to clear out your room and book your train home. Hand in your pass and uniform before you go, please." And with that he walks away with Mr Judge. The last few staff members wander away too, looking **shocked** at what they've just seen.

Poor Cleo is **sobbing** next to me. "Did that really just happen?" she asks.

"I think so," I say touching her arm. "They really think you did it."

"Anisha, you have to believe me, I didn't do this."

"I believe you," I say. "But it doesn't look good. Even if it's not your jacket, it fits like it is. We need to **PROVE** it isn't yours."

Cleo puts her head in her hands. "What a mess! I've lost my job, I won't be able to save the money for my space-camp trip and all my plans are totally ruined!"

"Okay, don't panic. You didn't do it, but someone else did...and if we find the owner of the jacket, we might be able to prove they did it and clear your name," I say.

"You really think we could?" Cleo asks hopefully.

"Well, maybe. We just need to figure out what we know for sure. Let me write this down," I say, grabbing a pen and scrap of paper Mr Judge left behind on the desk. My mind is whirring already. "Right, so the paint on the jacket was still wet, so whoever put it on the hook must have noticed the stain and dumped it in the staffroom quickly so that they weren't caught wearing it. They didn't factor in you coming along and picking it up."

I write down:

Jacket – unknown owner, smudged handprint. Must have been dumped after the damage to Delilah.

I also write down:

8.30 – saw Delilah, all fine

9.25 – Delilah damage discovered

That's a window of just an hour. In that time
someone vandalized Delilah, got rid of any evidence
and dumped the jacket in the staffroom.

"Can I borrow the jacket?" I ask. "It might be
helpful when I'm investigating. Trust me. I've had
a little bit of experience with **mystery-solving** in
the past."

"Yeah, of course – here," Cleo says, pulling off
the paint-stained garment. I check the label – the
size says medium. Cleo continues, "I'll get mine
cleaned and put away for now. We only get one
jacket, that's why I had to borrow the first one I
found. Thanks for trying to help, Anisha, I do really
appreciate it. I don't know how much luck you're

going to have though. I'd better go back to my room and phone my mum. She's going to be so **upset**."

"Don't worry," I say. "We won't let you take the **blame** for something you didn't do."

CHAPTER SEVEN

SKATING AND SKIDDING!

Cleo leaves to go back to her room and phone her mum while I sit on the grass, trying to think of what to do next. Just then Mindy walks up, munching chips.

"I thought I'd come and see how the interrogations went," she jokes.

"Not good," I say, not smiling. "Cleo got the blame and Tom fired her!"

"**WHAT?**" Mindy exclaims.

"**WHAT?**" another voice shouts behind her.

I peer round Mindy to see who the other person is. It's a girl, wearing a staff uniform and a name tag that says Rae.

"Hey," I say.

She kneels down. "What happened? They haven't even questioned everyone yet – I'm just going to see them now. That can't be right – Cleo can't be fired!" she says.

"I'm afraid it's true," I say.

"**NO!** This is all one big **disastrous** mistake!" Rae shrieks, then she jumps up and storms off.

"Okay, she was angry," Mindy says. "So, do you think Cleo did it?"

"No, definitely not. I want to help her, Mindy."

Mindy grins. "I was waiting for you to say that. Where do we start?"

"Well, I think another member of staff could be the culprit. They blamed Cleo because of the paint on her uniform jacket, but it wasn't her jacket. So we need to find out who is the same size as her to **narrow** down our list of suspects," I start. "And these jackets are only worn by the people in charge of the activities so that points to someone on that team."

"Okay, well, the boys are busy off doing their own thing – we can catch them up later. Why don't we try out some activities and try to get talking to the team that organize them? They all work with Cleo so they might know something that helps our investigation, and we can suss out who might fit the jacket at the same time," suggests Mindy. "We can grab a schedule from the activities tent."

My tummy dips at the thought of trying activities, but Cleo needs our help. I have to do whatever it takes – I just hope that won't include anything high up!

"Okay," I say. "I guess it's the best way. Let's go."

Now we have a **plan**, we practically run to the activities tent. It's already quite busy in there, but straight away I see Aunty Bindi in the art section. Well, actually, I see Uncle Tony first, looking surprisingly comfortable. He's wearing what looks like a cream bed sheet wrapped around him, pinned with a brooch. He's got a crown of leaves on his head and he's lying back on a chaise longue. He looks quite **regal** and like he's enjoying himself! He's surrounded by eight easels and behind them eight people attempting to paint him. The canvases I can see are all very different. One has a picture showing Uncle Tony with a big head and a tiny body. Another is Uncle Tony drawn as square blocks making up his body parts.

We walk over. "Dad?" Mindy shouts. "What are you dressed as? **So embarrassing!**"

Uncle Tony looks up. "Ah, hi, sweetheart. I'm a Roman emperor. I get to lie here and eat grapes and everyone paints me. It's much more fun than I thought it would be. Ooh, have you got chips?" He goes to grab one from Mindy's cone.

"Sweetums, no! You can't eat chips, that's not historically accurate!" Aunty Bindi squeals.

The other painters in the group sigh. The session leader, a woman, comes over. "Sorry, everyone. We can't have the life model moving around, it's very distracting for the artists."

"We didn't mean to disturb the session," I say. "Your life model is her dad," I explain, pointing to Mindy.

Aunty Bindi comes over. "This is my stepdaughter – I told you all about her. Mindy is a super-talented actress. And my stepson Manny isn't here right now, but he is so clever, he's a genius with anything techy." She beams. "This is my niece, Anisha, my little scientist, and her friend Milo is here somewhere too – he's part of the family. We take him everywhere with us, don't we, Anisha?"

I nod, hoping Aunty Bindi doesn't start giving this woman our whole family history. That's usually what she does when she meets new people, so introductions can take a while! But the woman is clearly keen to get the painting going again, and she just smiles and then turns her back on us.

"I'd better get back to it too," whispers Aunty Bindi, waving her paintbrush at us.

"Okay, can we take this schedule with us? We might try some activities." Mindy smiles and reaches for the schedule from Bindi's easel.

"Of course, Mindykins!" Bindi beams.

I have a quick look around at the activities staff in this tent to see if any of them could be suspects, but they all look far too small for the jacket.

"Let's try in the next tent," I say to Mindy. "We can find somewhere to sit and decide which activity to go to first."

It turns out it's the cooking tent, and Mum and Dad are in here taking a baking class. There are five

rows of counters, each with their own oven and two
people baking at each counter. At the front stands
a man wearing a headset and talking into the
microphone, giving them
instructions. As far as
I can see Mum
and Dad are
mostly giggling
and throwing
flour at each
other. Dad's
nose is all white
and Mum's hair is
sprinkled with it too.

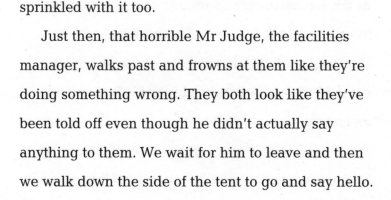

Just then, that horrible Mr Judge, the facilities
manager, walks past and frowns at them like they're
doing something wrong. They both look like they've
been told off even though he didn't actually say
anything to them. We wait for him to leave and then
we walk down the side of the tent to go and say hello.

"Ooh, hi, kids, having a nice time?" Dad asks as he whisks some eggs. "We're making brownies!"

"We're trying to figure out who **vandalized** Delilah," I say. "We're checking out some of the activities team. Somebody knows **something**."

"Now, Anisha, maybe this is one to stay out of," Mum warns. "This is our holiday – you should take a break and go find that reading nook Cleo mentioned," she says as she measures some cocoa powder out into a bowl.

"But it's **important**, Mum. Tom and Mr Judge think Cleo did it, but I'm sure she didn't. You wouldn't like it if I got the blame for something I didn't do, would you?" I remind her. "Remember when the school got flooded with foam?"

"Well, no, but...oh, what am I saying? You're going to try and **solve** this mystery whatever I say, aren't you? Can we do anything to help?" Mum asks.

"Thanks, Mum, we're good at the moment – we have a plan. You could keep an ear out for any park gossip though. We just don't know why **anyone** would want to damage such a beloved mascot of the park right before the big celebration."

"Maybe they don't like ducks," says Dad, stirring some butter in a pan on the small hob.

"I don't think it's that," I say, turning to my parents. "We'll see you later, Mum. Have fun, Dad. Save us some brownies!"

Outside, Mindy and I grab a seat and look at the park map and schedule.

"Look how many activities are going on!" Mindy exclaims.

"Okay, let's think **logically**," I say. "Who have we met so far who might be the same size as Cleo and might own that jacket?" And then I remember. "Cleo said she's friends with Rae, that girl who got upset when I said Cleo had been fired. Plus, Cleo mentioned she had Rae's jumper yesterday. She said they often borrow each other's clothes!"

"Okay, that's got to be worth checking out then,"

Mindy says, running her finger down the activities schedule to see where Rae is right now. Her finger stops.

"You've got to be **kidding me!**" I say.

"It's for Cleo," Mindy reminds me.

A few minutes later we're standing outside the roller-skate shack.

"We don't have to actually **try** it though, do we?" I say.

"We can't just go up to her and ask if she did it. We have to blend in and ask our questions in a non-suspicious way," Mindy points out.

"I hate it when you're right," I say.

There are a couple of other kids roller-skating round the ramp area and doing tricks. They make it look so easy. We get some roller skates from Rae, who seems to have calmed down now, but she gets called away by a kid who is struggling with their skates before we can talk to her about Delilah or the jacket. I do notice though that she is wearing a jacket, so maybe we're wrong about her and the jacket with the paint on it. Maybe it **doesn't** belong to her at all. We sit down on a bench to put our skates on.

"What's with these laces? Why are they so long?" I say.

Mindy grins. "Maybe this wasn't a good idea after all?"

I frown. "No, we've started now, we have to at least give it a try. Granny says we can do anything we set our minds to."

"That's true," agrees Mindy. "Let's do it."

We help each other up and for a second I think, **This is okay!** But then about a millisecond later, my legs start moving in opposite directions. "What the—" I say, as I'm somehow now doing the splits.

Mindy starts to laugh but then loses her balance and wobbles. She manages to catch herself by sticking out one arm and one leg to stabilize.

"Okay, grab my arm," she says. "We'll hold each other up. Look, those guys are doing it. We just have to ease into it."

"Okay," I say, unsure, grabbing Mindy's arm and holding on for **dear life**. "Let's try putting one foot in front of the other," I say.

So we move like that, slowly walk-sliding along. Every so often we wobble and manage to grab on to a tree or the railing that circles this bit of the park. Thankfully the path here is smooth, so that helps!

It's just as we're trying to do a longer run without holding anything that I spot him. It's that older kid from the entertainment team, Bobby! He's skating away from us and holding something wrapped in a yellow-paint-stained rag. Not just any yellow. From here it looks like the **exact yellow** that was splattered all over Delilah and smudged on the jacket Cleo was wearing. And he's looking around like he doesn't want to be seen.

"Psst, Mindy, look what Bobby's carrying. We have to follow him, **NOW!**" I whisper.

"What? Let's at least take off our roller skates then. I don't think we're ready for **whizzing** round the park yet," says Mindy.

Just then I see Dillon, also on roller skates. Where did he come from? He sees me, looks at Bobby and **smirks**. Quick as a flash, he goes after him. Is he planning another one of his daft pranks?

"There's no time," I say. "We'll lose him if we stop to do that, and look – Dillon is following him too, probably to play some silly prank, but it might interfere with vital evidence! We have to follow them both now!"

Mindy raises her eyebrow. "Okay, I guess. Let's just be careful!"

We move off and follow Dillon and Bobby along the path. We've gone a little way when Dillon turns to face us and sticks out his tongue. Then he dives behind a bush to hide, grabs a pebble from the floor and then deliberately throws it to make a noise so Bobby looks around. Dillon can see we're trying to follow Bobby discreetly – he's trying to **expose** us! Dillon disappears from view as Bobby looks back at us. Mindy and I look away, trying to appear preoccupied, like we're not following him at all.

"That's a lovely tree," I say loudly.

"Oh, yeah, lovely!" Mindy agrees enthusiastically, then we turn back to see Bobby skate on.

I look around. Dillon seems to have disappeared too – maybe he'll leave us alone now.

"Come on, let's keep following Bobby," I say. "He's fast; we'll have to speed up."

"I don't know if that's a good idea, Anisha," Mindy says.

"We'll hold onto each other," I reassure her.

"Look who's being adventurous!" Mindy laughs.

"I'm not really. I just want to prove Cleo is **innocent**," I reply.

"You really care, don't you? It's so great how you always stand up for what's right, Anisha," Mindy

says, linking arms with me as we move off again.
Just then there's a rustle in the bush next to us.
Before we can move away, Dillon jumps out,
shouting, **"BOO!"**

"Aaargh!" I shout. Mindy and I both stumble
backwards in fright, but our legs and skates get
tangled up and we fall awkwardly into a hedge, with
me landing on top of Mindy!

"Ouch!" she yelps.

"Oh no! I'm so sorry!" I say. I scramble off her then climb out of the bush and look around for Dillon to tell him off for scaring us, but he's nowhere to be seen – and neither is Bobby.

"My ankle – it really hurts. I need to get the boot off." Mindy groans. "Sorry, I guess we lost Bobby."

"Don't worry about that," I say. "I'm going to get some help, okay? Don't move."

I spot someone with the park uniform on back down the path.

"Excuse me?" I shout, waving to get their attention. "My friend has hurt herself – can you help?"

Mindy props herself up on her elbows. "Anisha, see if you can catch up with Bobby. There's no point us both being stuck here. I'll be fine."

"No way," I say. "First things first, we're getting that ankle looked at."

"It's really sore. I don't think I can walk on it. We need to let Dad and Bindi know. They're probably going to want to take me to the main building for a proper check – I might have to go to hospital." Mindy grimaces.

"This is all my **fault**. I got so focused on following Bobby, and now you're injured," I say.

"I didn't have to follow you, did I?" Mindy says. "It was an accident and it would have been fine if it wasn't for that annoying Dillon."

"I suppose," I say, but I still feel bad. Dillon is upsetting more than my mystery-solving and I don't like it one bit.

ANNOYING BOY
+
SILLY PRANKS
=
UNACCEPTABLE!

CHAPTER EIGHT

OVERHEARD!

The first-aider arrives and we get Mindy to the medical room, where the camp doctor checks her over. I try to use my radio to let the rest of the family know what's happened, but I can't get it to work, so I go with a member of staff to put out an announcement for Uncle Tony and Aunty Bindi to make their way here.

When I return to Mindy's bedside, her cheeks are really flushed.

"Are you okay?" I ask.

"I just overheard something!" she says.

"What was it?"

"It was to do with the paint!" Mindy says **excitedly** – but before she can say anything else, Aunty Bindi bursts into the room!

"Mindy, my precious, are you okay?" she squeals as she sits on the bed, grabs Mindy in a bear hug and basically smothers her.

"I'm fine," Mindy mumbles. "But I won't be if you don't let go in a bit!"

Bindi goes a bit pink and releases her grip on Mindy. "Sorry, precious, I was just so **frightened** when we heard the message to come here." She picks a twig out of Mindy's hair.

"Where's Dad?" Mindy asks.

Bindi notices Uncle Tony isn't here. "Oh, we came running out of the art class. He was right behind me and I did tell him to hurry up – no dawdling when it's life or death!"

"It wasn't life or death," Mindy tells her. "But I guess it's nice you were worried."

Uncle Tony comes in then. "Sweetums, you raced

off without me!" he moans at Bindi. He's still dressed
in a toga and has to keep flicking the long loose end
of the sheet over his shoulder. "Mindy sweetheart,
what happened?" he asks, concerned.

"Hi, Dad. I'm fine. I probably shouldn't try roller-
skating again for a bit though." She winks at me.
I know she's trying to make a joke of it all,
but I still feel bad about what happened.

The doctor steps forward. "Hi, I'm Doctor Mitch. Your daughter has been lucky. It's just a light sprain so she'll need to take it easy for a few days. No rock climbing or heavy exercise. I'll give her a crutch to use until the swelling goes down."

We're just getting Mindy up to try out the crutch when Milo and Manny burst in, out of breath.

"**Woah, sis!** What did you do?" Manny exclaims.

"Are you okay?" Milo asks. "I was having a lovely chat with a horse at the stables. Then I heard the message over the tannoy, and Manny and I both came running from the other side of the park! Why didn't you just use the radio?"

"I couldn't get it to work," I say.

"Anyway, I'm fine, I fell over on roller skates and sprained my ankle. No big deal," Mindy replies.

"Well, I don't want to say '**I told you so**' but if you'd done some combat training with me last week, I could have shown you how to fall without hurting yourself," Manny says knowingly.

"If you don't stop being a pain, I'll show you some combat training with this crutch!" warns Mindy.

"Now, **beta**," Uncle Tony interrupts. "No hitting your brother with your crutch, that's not nice."

Doctor Mitch speaks up again. "I think you're fine to take Mindy back to your lodge. We've got a buggy you can drive back over in. You won't all fit in there though, I'm afraid!"

Aunty Bindi takes charge. "Tony and I will drive Mindy back to the lodge and you kids can take your time – maybe go do another activity, grab lunch, explore a bit and then walk back. It's almost 11 a.m. Shall we say we'll meet back at the lodge for 5 p.m. and we can eat dinner together?"

"That's **seventeen hundred hours**," Manny interrupts.

"Yes, thank you, Manny. Right, sweetheart, let's get you in the buggy. Wow, I haven't said that for a long time!" Uncle Tony chuckles as he lifts Mindy off the bed.

"Ugh, Dad, it's not that kind of buggy!" Mindy protests but she lets him carry her anyway. We all follow them outside and watch as Mindy and Uncle Tony sit in the back of the golf buggy while Aunty Bindi gets in the driver's seat and tries to figure out the controls before they swerve away down the path towards the lodge.

"Do you think they'll be okay?" Manny asks.

"Umm, I'm sure they'll be fine," I say, not completely sure as Bindi beeps at the people on the path to get out of her way.

Mr Judge comes out of an office behind us and watches as Aunty Bindi just misses a tree. "I hope you're all staying out of trouble," he warns. "I think we've had enough **excitement** for one weekend."

We don't really know what to say, so we just nod. Mr Judge narrows his eyes at us and then strides away. He is a very strange man.

"What now?" Milo asks. "I don't really feel like doing an activity."

"You can show me how to **work** this radio," I say.

"Did you turn this dial at the top?" asks Manny.

My face feels hot. "Umm, no. Okay, thank you!" I say, quickly taking the radio back.

Just then Mindy's voice comes over on the radio: *"Anisha, are you there?"*

I look at Manny, and he signals for me to press the talk button.

"Yeah, I'm here. Are you okay?" I ask.

"Yeah – ouch, careful! Bindi's driving is a bit wild, but we're almost at our lodge so that's one good

thing," Mindy says. *"Anyway, I realized I didn't finish telling you what I overheard while I was in the medical room."*

"Oh yeah, what was it?" I ask, leaning into the radio to listen. Manny and Milo do the same.

"Well, two of the park staff were talking, and one of them was saying how they couldn't find any of the yellow face paint for the kids' body art workshop and the other one said that couldn't be right, as they'd only just had an order of supplies delivered. Anisha, do you think the paint on Delilah could be face paint?"

"It could be, I guess – if it was in a squeezy tube, then maybe. I need to go back and look at Delilah, I think."

Mindy groans as it sounds like the buggy comes to a screeching stop. *"Okay, I'll talk to you in a bit. We've just got back to the lodge."*

"Okay, take it easy, Mindy. Rest up and we'll see you in a while," I say.

Milo looks at me. "What's going on, Neesh? It sounds like you're investigating without us."

"Well, kind of, but I didn't mean to. Let me explain and it'll make sense."

So I go through what happened: how Cleo got the blame for vandalizing Delilah, but how it wasn't her jacket at all. I explain how we were roller-skating and then saw Bobby, but Dillon got in the way and scared us so I fell on Mindy and that's how she got hurt.

"It's not your fault, Anisha. If Dillon hadn't scared you both, you wouldn't have dived in the bush and Mindy wouldn't have sprained her ankle. What's his **problem**, anyway?" Manny asks.

"I don't know. He just thinks it's funny to **prank** people. We need to get him to stop, but I don't know how," I say, frustrated.

"We'll help. You know we've got your back, Neesh." Milo smiles.

"Yeah, no one messes with our family," Manny agrees.

"Okay, so we need a plan. Bobby definitely had
a paint-stained rag earlier, and although it might be
nothing, it's a lead, so I think we should follow it up.
We'll deal with Dillon as well; I just need to think
about how. In the meantime, let's return to the scene
of the crime."

When we get there, Tom the manager is standing
in front of the giant duck and talking to a woman in
overalls.

"There must be **something** we can do to speed
things up, Jo. We can't have the celebration without

the sculpture, it's the
centrepiece to the
whole thing!"
Tom says.

I nudge Milo.
"Jo? Who is she?"

"I guess she
could be the
maintenance person.

Maybe she's worth talking to about the paint!" Milo whispers.

Jo frowns at Tom. "I'm afraid not. Delilah needs a whole new wing! That would take time to make. We don't have any more of the fabric we used so we'd have to order more and it takes a week to come!" she replies, before walking off to her truck nearby.

Tom shakes his head in despair. "This can't be happening!" he mutters.

"Wait here!" I say to the others and I run after Jo.

"Excuse me!" I call out. "Could I just ask a question?"

Jo turns around. "Oh, hello. Course you can, though I'm not sure I'll know the answer. The entertainment staff usually know a lot more than me about what's on," she says, smiling.

"Oh, no, it's not about that. I was wondering about what happened to Delilah. The yellow paint on her feathers – is that a colour you keep here on site?"

"Actually, no. I had a good look at that and it's

not metal or woodwork paint. I think it's craft paint or maybe even face paint," Jo says.

"**Face paint?** Like what they had at the barbecue?" I ask.

"Yep, just like that. But I can't believe what they're all saying – that Cleo did it? She seems so nice," Jo says.

"Yeah, I don't believe she did it either," I say. "Thanks so much for your help!"

I run back to the others, who are talking to Tom.

"Isn't the party meant to be on Bank Holiday Monday? That's only the day after tomorrow!" Milo says.

Tom grimaces. "Well yes. I don't know what we're going to do if Jo can't fix Delilah though."

"We'll think of something," Milo says brightly.

"That's a problem for us to solve, not for you to worry about. Anyway, are you all okay, can I help you with anything?" Tom asks.

"We just wanted to see Delilah again." I smile.

"Okay, well I've got a meeting with Mr Judge and the rest of the team, so I'd better get on."

We say goodbye to Tom and then sit down on the grass near Delilah. I look up at her, trying to see any clue of how this happened to her. I think out loud.

"So, the paint on Delilah could be craft or face paint," I say. "And that ties in with what Mindy overheard about the missing face paint."

"So, we know what was used, but not who used it," Milo says.

"Well, we need to look into Bobby, and also find out who has access to the supply cupboard where the face paint is kept. Hopefully those two things will bring us a bit closer to figuring this whole thing out," I say. "Cleo might be able to help us – we should go and see her."

"Okay, let's go," Manny says, pulling me up.

Milo stands too, looks up at the duck sculpture and says, "We won't let you down, Delilah."

CHAPTER NINE

MYSTERY OF THE MISSING WING

It's nearly lunchtime now and I can hear Milo's tummy growling as we walk.

We grab some chips and walk round to the staff lodges. Cleo had told me where they were, just in case I needed her. When we get there, Cleo is sitting outside on the doorstep, talking on the phone. She looks **upset**.

"Yes, Mum, I know, I tried to tell them," she says, waving at us to come and sit too.

"No, Mum, I don't need you to come here and tell my boss he's wrong. Listen, I've got to go, my friends are here, I'm hoping they can help me sort all this out, okay?" She pauses, listening. "What friend? Her name is Anisha. No, you haven't met her, I only just met her!" Then she sighs and holds the phone towards me. "She wants to talk to you. Sorry," Cleo apologizes.

I take the phone cautiously. "Hello?"

"Hello, dear – Anisha, is that your name?" Cleo's mum asks.

"Yes, Anisha," I reply.

"Well, Anisha, I want to say thank you for helping my daughter. She's a good girl and I know she didn't vandalize that duck. You do whatever you can, please, as she loves that job."

"I will," I promise, even though I have no idea if or how I'm going to be able to help.

Cleo says goodbye to her mum and sighs. "That's the **third time** she's phoned me since it happened."

"Our stepmum worries too; she would be even worse, I think!" Manny says.

"How are you all doing anyway?" Cleo asks us. "I don't suppose you've got any news?" she adds hopefully.

So, we fill Cleo in on everything we've seen and heard so far.

Seeing Bobby with a paint-stained rag wrapped around something and following him.

The news about the missing face paint + confirmation that it's face paint on Delilah.

Cleo sucks in a breath. "Do you think we've got enough to go to Tom and Mr Judge with?"

I shake my head. "No, because we don't really have anything concrete."

Cleo nods sadly. "It's so frustrating, because I know I didn't do it, but I can't prove it."

"Well, at least we have a suspect. Is there anything you can tell us about Bobby?" Manny asks.

"Well, I don't really know him that well. I haven't been here long enough really. He seems to get told off a lot by Tom though."

"Who's in charge of supplies for the activities the team run?" Milo asks. "Like the face paint, for example?"

Cleo raises an eyebrow. "Actually, it's Bobby. He holds the key to that cupboard, so if any of us need anything, we have to go to him."

"He's looking more and more like a **prime suspect**," I say.

"So now what?" Manny asks.

"Well, we need to actually talk to him," I begin. "Let's look at the schedule and see where he is at the moment."

We see that Bobby should be in the activities tent right now so I guess that's where we're going next.

"What can I do in the meantime?" asks Cleo. "I really appreciate you doing all this for me. I wish I could help more, but if Tom sees me wandering round the park, I'll probably end up in even more **trouble**!"

"Research," I say. "You have a laptop, right? Can you find out how we could make a new wing for Delilah? If we can help restore her, then at least the celebration can go ahead."

Cleo smiles. "Okay, good idea – and thanks for giving me a job to do. It's really **boring** being stuck here. I just keep thinking about space camp and what if I can't go now."

"Don't worry, we're going to prove you're innocent. Oh, and in the meantime, we should bring Mindy to come and sit with you tomorrow!" Manny says. "She's sprained her ankle so she can't walk on it much, but you could keep each other company."

"That would be lovely," Cleo agrees.

We make our way to the activities tent but there's no sign of Bobby and none of the other staff know where he is either. **Very suspicious.** We go for a little wander round the park to see if we can spot him, which we don't but we end up way out by the horses. Milo introduces us and they're so lovely we get a bit distracted and before I know it, it's time to start heading back.

It's almost 5 p.m. when we get back to the lodge. I can already smell Granny's cooking wafting out into the forest as we approach.

"I'm so hungry," Milo says.

"Me too," Manny agrees. "Now normally if we were sleeping out in the forest we'd have to forage for grubs and bugs for dinner, but I guess since Granny cooked it would be rude not to eat what she's made."

Milo and I laugh but then realize Manny is serious.

"Manny, have you ever really eaten bugs?" Milo asks. "I watched a documentary once about that. They said we should all try it, as bugs are rich in protein."

"**Urgh**, I'd rather eat sprouts than eat bugs!" I say.

We walk into the lodge just as Mum and Dad are telling everyone about their baking lesson. Aunty Bindi and Uncle Tony are sitting either side of a rather squished Mindy, who looks like she wants to escape but can't. Granny is of course in the kitchen, but because it's all open-plan she can listen too.

"So I mixed all the ingredients just like the instructor said, but somehow my brownies turned out like rock cakes," Dad moans.

"I did tell you not to turn the oven up so high," Mum says. "Anyway, what are we trying next?"

Dad huffs. "Nothing, I'm staying here tomorrow with my newspaper. Maybe I'll keep Mindy company."

Mindy looks horrified at that suggestion, so I jump in. "Actually, our friend Cleo said she needs some help with some...**umm**...crafts," I blurt out. "Mindy could still rest her leg, but it would get her out of the lodge."

"Isn't Cleo the girl who was accused of damaging the duck?" Uncle Tony asks. "And I was going to stay here with my Mindy – I thought we could have a movie marathon."

"Ooh, I'll stay, we can watch Bollywood films **ALL DAY**!" Aunty Bindi squeals and pinches Mindy's cheeks excitedly and grabs her in a bear hug.

Mindy shakes her head at me and draws the letters **SOS** in the air behind Aunty Bindi's back. So I say, "Well, it is the same girl, Uncle, but you know, I really don't think she did it. She had no reason to and being fired means she loses her opportunity to pay for her place at space camp. I don't think she would put that at risk. And anyway, we don't want Mindy getting stiff from sitting down **ALL** the time – she needs some movement, like the doc said. Plus, the fresh air will do her good. **AND** it means you and Aunty Bindi can do another activity together. Don't worry, I'll look after Mindy, I promise."

Mum, Dad, Uncle Tony and Aunty Bindi all look at me and then burst out laughing.

"What's so funny?" I ask.

"It's okay, we know Mindy wouldn't want to spend all day with the grown-ups – I just thought we'd have a little fun with you and pretend she had to," Uncle Tony chuckles.

"I wasn't joking." Aunty Bindi sulks. "But fine,

as long as we can watch one Bollywood film in the evening."

Mindy laughs. "Alright, alright, but not one where everyone's crying through the whole film."

Bindi thinks for a moment. "Okay, well I brought ten DVDs with me, there must be one in there you'll like."

"Great, now that's agreed, who's going to help me serve out the food?" Granny interrupts.

For the first time, I look at Granny properly. She's wearing a giant badge that says,

Top Archer!

"What's that, Granny?" I ask.

Granny beams proudly. "You like it? I was the best archer in my class today. The instructor said I have a very good eye. I told him I have **two** very good eyes,

thank you. I got the highest score out of everyone in my group. The instructor said he hasn't seen a score that high for ages! He gave me this badge. I think I'll wear it all the time."

"It's brilliant, Granny!" I say, smiling. My granny is always full of surprises.

"I might try fencing tomorrow, that looks fun. And have you seen the swimming dome? They have the biggest slide. I was a very good swimmer when I was a young girl, you know – faster than all my friends," she says. "And I really want to try the **zip wire!**"

Dad looks concerned. "Mum, a zip wire? Do you think that's a good idea? Maybe we could try a bit of pottery together instead?"

"Pah, pottery! That's not very adventurous, is it?" Granny huffs. "No thank you, I'm trying fencing and then I saw they have these quad bike thingies, and then I think we should all go swimming together. Family swim race!" She grins **mischievously**.

Dad looks like he might be sick, but says nothing.

He knows better than to tell Granny she can't do what she wants.

We lay the table with plates, cutlery and mats for the hot serving dishes and saucepans. I don't know how Granny does it, but even here in the forest she has served up a feast. There's chicken, rice, naan, potatoes, okra* and raita. It all looks delicious. We sit down and dig in. Mindy gets to sit on the sofa because of her ankle, so I go and sit with her.

"How are you feeling?" I ask.

"Not too bad. Don't tell Bindi and Dad, but it's not as painful as it was earlier. I quite like them running round after me." She giggles.

"Mindy!" I say, but I'm smiling too. "They do go a bit over the top, don't they?"

"Dad offered to rub my feet earlier," Mindy says. "I told him that's taking it too far. Anyway, what's the real plan for tomorrow? I know you have one."

---

* Okra are also called lady fingers. Granny calls them bhinda, which always makes me smile because it sounds a bit like Bindi, my aunty! Raita is a lovely minty yoghurt that Granny makes. Sometimes she puts in shredded cucumber too! SO tasty!

"Well, we talked to Cleo and realized that Bobby could definitely have done it. He had the paint-stained rag, but he's also **in charge** of the supply cupboard where they keep the face-paint tubes **AND** we know from the conversation you overheard that a load of face paint went missing."

"Sounds like an open and shut case." Mindy whistles.

"Well, it kind of does, but I'm wondering if that's too simple. And besides, we still don't know why anyone would want to damage Delilah. More investigating is needed before we can accuse Bobby. I'm not sure that jacket Cleo was wearing would fit him either. He's quite short, I think. Anyway, we're going to try and talk to him tomorrow at whatever activity he's running. You can help Cleo with ideas for repairing Delilah's wing, because they're not going to be able to get a new one in time for the party." I take a breath.

"Er...do you think you took on a bit too much?" Mindy asks.

"No, we can do it, we just need to **focus** –
and avoid that Dillon boy. He keeps getting in the
way and I'm still mad you got hurt in the process,"
I grumble.

"Anisha, I don't like him much either, but I was
thinking, maybe he keeps hanging around us
because he's **lonely**. You know, we all have each
other, but he really doesn't seem to have anyone.
I remember how that feels. I know I've always had
Manny but he's my twin and super annoying a lot of
the time, so that doesn't count. You're my first real
friend and it's so lovely what we have."

I think for a second. When she puts it like that,
I feel bad for Dillon. "You might be right, I guess.
Still, if he's trying to make friends, he's not doing a
very good job," I say.

"Maybe he doesn't know how. I didn't," Mindy
reminds me.

"Alright, I'll try to talk to him," I promise.

Just then there's a commotion over the other side

of the room and Aunty Bindi squeals, "**DUCK!**"

We all crouch down and duck our heads immediately. "What is it?" I shout. "Is it a wasp? Where is it?"

"No, actual **DUCKS!**" Aunty Bindi screams, pointing at the glass doors at the back of the lodge.

"Calm down, sweetums, they can't get inside – the patio door is closed," Uncle Tony says.

I get up and look where Aunty Bindi is pointing. It's the ducks from yesterday again. They are standing in a line outside the doors like they're waiting to be let in.

"I wonder why they came back. We already got them out once," Manny says.

"They are brave cheeky little duckies!" Granny Jas giggles.

"Shall we let them in? It feels a bit rude leaving them out there," Milo says. "I could ask them what they want."

"Milo, no!" we all shout.

"Oh, well I'll go out to them then," Milo decides.

He slides the patio door open and shuts it quickly behind him. The ducks waddle backwards a bit but don't leave. Milo crouches down so he's on their level and tries to get them to come closer by reaching out his hand.

"This could go very wrong," Manny says. "Maybe I should have gone out there. My survival skills include defending yourself against—"

"Ducks?" Dad finishes with a smile.

"Not just ducks, Uncle, but yes, ducks can become territorial and aggressive if they feel threatened," Manny says with an air of importance, like he's the authority on ducks.

Milo is now leaning closer to the one who looks like the mama duck. I can hear him making clucking and squawking noises* and weirdly the duck seems to be squawking back. It's almost like they're having a conversation! Milo smiles and then comes back in, saying to the ducks as he closes the door, "Just wait there, I'll be back!"

"Everything okay, Milo?" Mum asks as she gets up to grab some more rice.

"Well, I think they keep coming back this way because they are trying to get to the water," Milo says. "I was reading that some ducks make the same trip every year after they have their ducklings. Maybe they've got a bit lost."

"That makes sense, Milo – look!" says Manny as he taps busily on his phone. He holds it up to show us the screen. "I'm sure I heard someone say earlier that these are the newer lodges – they haven't been here that long. The ducks are probably confused."

✿★✿☆✿✿★✿✿✿★✿✿★✿☆★✿☆✿★✿★✿✿✿★✿✿

* If you didn't already know, Milo thinks he has Animal Intuition – he says he can understand animals. Now I didn't used to believe it but recently I'm thinking he might actually have it!

"Shouldn't the park staff have thought of that, though?" I ask. "Surely they would know if there's a family of ducks living here."

"Yeah, but there's a lot of wildlife in the park, Neesh, easy to miss one little family of ducks. I think we need to help them."

"How?" Mindy asks from the sofa.

"I can guide them to the lake," Milo says gleefully.

"You could be like the Pied Piper of ducks!" Dad grins.

"Well, I'm staying out of the way. There's something about those ducks that makes me a bit squeamish," says Aunty Bindi.

"How will you get them to follow you?" asks Uncle Tony. "Maybe with seeds?"

"It worked when we used lettuce to get them out before," says Milo. "We'll need to make sure the little ducks don't get hurt or left behind. I might need your help, everyone. I'm going to do some research. Manny, can I borrow your tablet?"

"Yeah, sure, I'll help," says Manny. "We might have to go upstairs though; the signal seems to be better up there."

"Okay, can we take our food up with us, Granny?" Milo asks.

"Yes, yes, only this time though!" says Granny. "I don't know, you kids, always on some sort of important mission. Who is going to sweep all those duck feathers off the patio, that's what I want to know? And they left lots of fluff in here when they came yesterday too. So cute when they flap their wings but so messy!"

Something makes me stop when Granny says that. I think for a moment. The ducks left feathers behind when they flapped their wings. Flapping wings. **WINGS!**

I turn to Mindy. "Delilah had two wings, now she only has one. Where did the other one go?"

Mindy shrugs. "I guess the vandal took it with them or threw it away?"

"Exactly!" I say. "If Bobby has the wing, then that proves he did it! We have to **find that wing!**"

Later that night, as we're all climbing into bed, I go to close the curtains and happen to look across at the lodge next door. I see Dillon. He's sitting by his window too. Downstairs I can see his parents laughing and having a glass of wine. I look back up at Dillon; he seems bored.

Maybe Mindy is right; maybe he is just lonely. Just then he notices me. He looks surprised so I smile, but he sticks his tongue out at me and then pulls the curtain across. **RUDE!**

CHAPTER TEN

LOOK UP!

The next day is Sunday. The party is supposed to be tomorrow. We have a lot to do before then:

1. Find the missing wing, investigate Bobby, hopefully prove who vandalized Delilah and clear Cleo's name.

2. Avoid Dillon and his pranks!

3. Find a way to repair or replace Delilah's wing.

4. Help Milo get the ducks to the water safely.

5. In between all that, somehow do all the activities Granny wants to do!

Phew, I hope we can do it. Plus, it would be nice to wrap all this up and actually get some chill-out time in the reading nook. This was supposed to be a holiday!

After breakfast everyone heads out of the lodge. Granny goes to try fencing, Mum and Dad decide they're going to do pottery together, while Uncle Tony and Aunty Bindi are hiring Segways and exploring the park. We all agree to meet up at the swimming dome in two hours from now.

"Segways require balance, Dad, are you sure you'll be okay?" Manny asks.

"Yeah, I can stand upright, son," Uncle Tony says, just as he almost falls over trying to put his shoes on.

"I'll look after him," says Aunty Bindi. "We'll be fine – it's just like riding a bike, right?"

"Well, not really," starts Mindy, but they're already out the door.

I look at Milo, Mindy and Manny. "Okay,

we have to make today count. Let's check the park schedule and see where Bobby is this morning."

We pull out the schedule.

DAY	A.M	P.M	LEADER
FRI	WELLY WANGING	ROLLER SKATING	RAE
SAT	ULTIMATE TWISTER	FANCY DRESS RELAY	CLEO
SUN	OUTDOOR CRAFTS	HUMAN JENGA	BOBBY
MON	PIE-EATING CONTEST	MAKE A POTATO CHARACTER	JAMIL

It says that Bobby is running an outdoor craft workshop this morning.

"Okay," I say, "we'll take Mindy to Cleo's lodge so they can try and figure out how to make Delilah a new wing. While they're doing that, we'll investigate Bobby at the outdoor craft workshop. Can you make it as far as Cleo's lodge, Mindy?"

"I'm okay, I think. I feel quite steady with the

crutch and I'm still pretty fast," Mindy says proudly.

"Not faster than me!" Manny challenges.

"I'm not racing you, Manny. Do I look like I want to fall over again?" Mindy tells him.

"Hey, Neesh, if this Bobby did do it, I wonder why? It's such a weird thing to do," Milo remarks.

"Maybe ducks make him angry?" Mindy suggests.

"But they're so **cute!**" Milo argues.

"Maybe it's not Bobby after all, but a bunch of rebel resident ducks who are offended by the inaccurate nature of Delilah's likeness to actual ducks!" Manny says very seriously.

"What?!" Mindy snorts. "Manny, do **YOU** even know what you mean?"

"Laugh all you want! The forest is a dark and dangerous place!" Manny says meaningfully.

"Stop, guys, we do need a serious motive," I say. "Plus, I'm not sure the resident ducks could carry a tube of paint or rip off a wing, Manny," I say.

"Okay, then what other ideas do you lot have?" Manny huffs, adjusting his camouflage-patterned survival headband.

"Well, let's just get to this workshop and see if we've got a proper suspect first. Hopefully he'll give something away accidentally when we talk to him. He definitely had the means and opportunity to do it as he had access to the paint. But we can't just walk up to him and ask him if he did it, because he'll probably just say no. So we've got to be subtle, okay? The best thing would be if we can get a look inside the supply cupboard! That way we can check out where the face paint was kept. And could you imagine if the missing wing is in there?"

Milo grins. "I love it when we investigate. Super stealth-mode activated!"

"If we're going undercover maybe we should wear camouflage," Manny offers. "I have some stuff in my survival kit we could use."

After we've dropped Mindy off with Cleo, Milo, Manny and I walk round to the area outside the activities tent where Bobby is setting up the crafts workshop. There are no other kids here yet, so we offer to help. Bobby hesitates but then agrees.

"You can lay out the paper, pens and scissors on each place," he says, pointing to a pile of supplies on a nearby table.

"What are we making?" I ask.

"**Umm**...animal masks," Bobby replies, but he seems distracted.

"Won't we need colour? Paint or felt-tips?" Milo asks.

"What? Oh yeah, they're in the supply cupboard. I'll unlock it," Bobby says.

This is what we were hoping for – a look inside the craft supply cupboard. I follow Bobby and, luckily, it's right near to the outdoor craft area. It's more of a small shed than a cupboard – tall and narrow, with lots of shelves on both walls all the way up to the ceiling.

"Wow," I say. "This is a crafter's dream. You have everything in here." I look around as I talk, trying to spot any

142

sign of the missing wing. But I can't see it in there.

"Yeah, the felt-tips and paint palettes are there on the low shelf," Bobby mutters.

"Oh, okay," I say, grabbing the supplies. "How about those up there?" I point to the highest shelf, where there is a row of paint tubes. Red, blue, green... Interestingly, I'm pretty sure there is a gap where I imagine the yellow tubes used to be.

"No, they're face paints, but I can't reach up there anyway."

"Don't you have a stepladder or something?" I ask, looking around for one.

Bobby looks annoyed. "No, it broke. I've been waiting for a replacement but as usual it's taking ages for our order to arrive. I have to ask someone to reach those down for me." He stops talking suddenly like he's said too much. "We'd better get back," he says abruptly and stands by the door, waiting for me to walk out.

We rejoin the others and Bobby starts signing in some of the kids who have arrived.

"Anything interesting in the shed, Neesh?" Milo whispers as we move round the tables, putting felt-tips out.

"Yeah, a big gap where the yellow face paint should be. But we might have a problem with our theory. Bobby is too short to reach that shelf."

"He could have used a stepladder or a stool," Manny points out.

"He said it broke and he has to ask someone to get stuff down for him, but then he just **clammed up** and wouldn't talk any more," I explain.

"Hmm, maybe he's just saying that to throw you off?" says Milo.

"Maybe. I just feel like I'm missing something," I reply.

"Let's do the activity and see if he gives anything else away," Manny suggests.

So we sit down at a table and listen as Bobby

gives instructions on how to make the animal masks. Milo and Manny really get into it. Milo makes a duck mask, of course, and Manny makes an odd camouflage-patterned creature, which he says is so good at disguising itself we don't know what it is!

Bobby grunts at that when he comes round to look at what we've made. Mine is only half done – it's a peacock.

"You can stay a bit longer to finish it, if you want," Bobby offers. Why is he being nice now?

But before I can answer, Granny Jas arrives. "Come on, kids, you'll **love** this next activity," she says.

"What is it?" I ask. Granny is dressed very strangely. She's wearing a jumpsuit, which suggests an adventurous activity. That makes my tummy turn.

Granny grins gleefully. "**ZIP WIRE!**" she says.

"Er, I don't think so," I say.

"Nonsense, you'll have the best view in the park, plus you'll be with Granny – what's not to like?" Granny insists, taking my hand. "You want to come too, **beta**?" she asks Bobby, who looks horrified.

"Um, no thank you. I have to work, plus I'm afraid of heights. Have you seen how high it is?

REALLY HIGH! So, er…no, I won't be doing that!" he mutters and walks away.

I look at Milo and Manny. "So, he couldn't have reached the top shelf even with a ladder because he's afraid of heights. It must have been someone else."

"We're back to where we started!" Manny moans.

"Not necessarily," Milo points out. "We know where the paint came from, right? Maybe having a look at the park from a different point of view will help us see what we're missing."

"You don't mean…?" I start.

"Yep, the zip wire will give us a view of the whole park." Milo nods. "We might be able to see a route the culprit could have taken."

"Ooh, **sky surveillance!**" Manny squeals.

"Come on, children, we'll never fit it in before our swim if we don't get a move on, eh!" Granny urges.

"Ohhh, I don't like this – I don't like it one bit!" I say, but I still follow.

CHAPTER ELEVEN

FLYING GRANNY!

"Are you having a good break, Granny?" Milo asks. "You're doing loads of activities."

"I'm living my best life! You should try it!" Granny Jas grins. "What's that thing you youngsters say? You don't want to get **FOMOO**, do you?"

"**FOMOO?** Oh, do you mean **FOMO?**" I giggle. "Fear of missing out? No, I don't have that at all. I'd be very happy to miss this one out!" I say.

As we walk to the dreaded zip wire, I ask Granny, "How are you so adventurous and I'm not. My dad's not either. Was Grandad adventurous?"

Granny looks at me. "He was just like you, Anni. He loved reading and learning, always talking about something new he had read. We were so different, but we made a good team. If he was here now he would be in that reading nook. But I'll tell you, there was this one time when we were much younger, before we had your father. We'd gone to the park and we were flying a kite. It got stuck in a tree, so I decided to climb up and get it. But I miscalculated and got stuck. Your grandfather, he hated heights, but he climbed right up to help me. You have his courage, Anni. **Beta**, you don't think it, but you **are** adventurous. You don't have to climb up high or whizz round on wheels to be adventurous. You step out of your comfortable place all the time! You are brave and help others when they need it."

I blush. "I'm a bit scared about the zip wire, Granny, but I think it might help us figure out who destroyed Delilah. If I can just see how far apart some of the places in the park are, it might help me work out who could have done it in the time we were at breakfast. I just wish this wasn't the best way to do that."

"Well, I'll be there with you and if you **really** don't want to do it when you get up there, no one is going to force you, okay?" She pats my shoulder.

"We'll be there too," Manny says.

"Yeah, don't forget us! This is going to be so **cool!**" Milo adds.

Hearing about my grandfather gives me a boost and suddenly I feel like I can do this.

We reach the kiosk at the start of the zip wire. The boy there gives us jumpsuits like the one Granny is wearing. "I have my own special custom-made jumpsuit. I've been jumping off things since before you were born, **beta**," she tells him proudly.

"You need one of these as well." The boy sighs. "Unless you have a custom-made harness too."

It takes a minute or fifteen to get into our harnesses – lots of straps and bits to click in. At one point Manny and Milo seem to be connected, which I'm sure is not right. Eventually everyone is in their own harness and jumpsuit and we start the climb up the steep stairway.

At the top we find ourselves on a long wooden platform which ends abruptly just a few metres in front of us. Before that there's a metal hook that hangs down from what must be the zip wire. There's a girl in charge up here, attaching people to the big hook. My tummy turns about five somersaults.

We watch the other people in the group going off the platform and down the wire. Some scream (which makes me feel even more nervous), some laugh and some even stick their arms out like they're flying!

Finally, it's Granny's turn and she steps forward. I look around us – we're **so high up!** Down below is the lake, shimmering and shining in the morning sun. A bird flies past, too close for my liking.

"Oh, I can't do it!" I say suddenly.

"It's not your turn yet anyway, beta. I'll show you how it's done and then you can follow, okay?" Granny says.

"Nope, I don't think that's going to work," I say. "I'll just go back down and wait for you all."

"But, Neesh – the investigation! You said you needed to see the whole park. We need to figure out how the culprit managed to get paint from the supply cupboard, damage Delilah and get away while we were having breakfast!" Milo reminds me.

The girl running the zip wire leans forward. "You could go together if you like. Tandem zip wire."

Granny squeals. "**YES!** We'd love to! Come on, beta, this is perfect!"

"Umm...I'm not sure," I start to say, but it's too late. I'm being attached to Granny and to the zip wire. Now Granny is in front and I'm holding onto her for dear life.

"You can relax your grip. You won't fall off," the girl operating the zip wire tells me.

I just nod – I can't speak.

"You've got this, Anisha!" Manny and Milo cheer me on as Granny and I shuffle along to the edge of the platform.

"Right, are we ready?" says the girl, tugging on Granny's harness to make sure it's secure. "Look straight ahead as you step off the platform. You can let go and spread your arms out, but don't be wiggling around and doing anything silly. You'd be surprised what people try to do once they're in the air."

"This is so much fun!" Granny giggles.

"Are you sure about this, Granny?" I ask nervously as we shuffle forward a little more.

Granny nods. "**No pain, no gain, beta!**" And just like that she steps off the platform and suddenly we're whizzing down the zip wire at a terrific speed. I hear her whooping as we fly through the air across the lake, our jumpsuits billowing in the breeze. I never imagined I'd do this, but once I get over the scary bit of stepping off the platform, I quite enjoy it!

Granny shouts,
"Oh look, **beta**, more
of those ducks, like
the ones that came
into our lodge!"

I look down too and
she's right, there are some
ducks paddling in the lake right
by some reeds. Maybe that's where our ducks have
been trying to get to. I must remember to tell Milo.

I look around as we travel along the zip wire.
When we slow down a little in the middle, I can see
the whole park!

There's Delilah!

And the main building.

There's the outdoor exercise equipment.

There's where we went for the barbecue.

I see the roller skating and the outdoor crafts.

I realize it's quite a way from the supply shed to

Delilah. Whoever did it must have been moving fast to have done it in the time it took for us to eat our breakfast! Oh, look, it's that stilt walker, standing near the activities tent. What was his name? Jamil!

Granny sees him too. "He's a tall boy. Maybe I should get some stilts? I could reach the top shelves in the kitchen then," Granny yells as we whizz to the other side of the lake.

That's when it hits me.

"Granny, you're a **genius!**" I shout, punching the air. "I know exactly where we need to investigate next!"

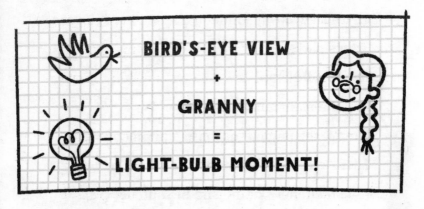

BIRD'S-EYE VIEW
+
GRANNY
=
LIGHT-BULB MOMENT!

CHAPTER TWELVE

GOING FOR A DIP

Granny and I wait for Manny and Milo to come across on the zip wire. They do it separately, both shouting and cheering as they whip across the lake.

"That was **AMAZING!**" Milo puffs, out of breath from shouting.

"Literally the best thing I've ever done!" agrees Manny. "And did you see, Anisha, how big the space is between the supply shed and Delilah?"

"Yes," I say. "Whoever it was, they moved fast."

"Well, we need to move fast now if we're going to make it to our swim," Granny Jas says, stepping out of her harness.

"But we just have to—" I start, but Granny gives me that look that says, *No. Just no.*

As we walk at Granny speed, which is very quick, I tell Milo and Manny what I thought of when I was up on the zip wire.

"So, remember how we said Bobby couldn't have reached the yellow face-paint tubes because he's too short and scared of heights? Well, what if there's someone here who **IS** tall enough to reach them?"

"Who?" Milo asks.

"The stilt walker – Jamil," I say. "Bobby said he asks someone to reach stuff down for him. It could be him."

"Maybe," says Manny.

"But he was by the outdoor exercise equipment when we saw him on our way to breakfast," Milo points out.

"Yeah, we need to check how long it would take to get from there to the supply shed and then to Delilah," I say.

"Less chatting, more speed!" says Granny.
"We'll miss our slot for the swimming pool."

"We'll talk after the swim and come up with
a plan," I tell Milo and Manny.

When we reach the swimming dome, Mum is
waiting outside the changing rooms.

"Right, kids, got your swimming costumes?" she asks.

We all look at each other. "Uh, no," I say.

Mum rolls her eyes and then laughs. "Good job
I remembered then, isn't it?" And she chucks three
towels and three sets of swim stuff at us. "Go and get
changed!" she chuckles.

There's a big family changing area with lots of
cubicles and rows of lockers. The floor is wet and there
are little kids running around squealing everywhere,
hairdryers blasting and parents calling out to their
children to stay still. I grab a cubicle, shut the door
behind me, lock it and sit down on the bench.

Swimming is **not** my favourite thing. There,
I said it. There are lots of things I don't like about it,
actually. I hate people who splash too close to you.
I don't like getting my face in the water and I can't
stand when you dry off afterwards but your hair is

still wet and it all drips down your neck! **Yuk!** But Mum always said it's important to have as a life skill and she insisted I take lessons, so I learned. I never got any certificates, but I can do a little bit of a paddle with my head out of the water and that's enough for me. Anyway, I don't go often, but since Granny Jas wants us all to do it together, I guess I can just sit on the side and dip my feet in the water. It'll be okay, won't it?

I get changed and come out of the cubicle, walk over to the row of lockers and find an empty one to put my stuff in. I put on the wristband that is attached to the locker key and I'm ready.

Milo and Manny whizz past me in their swim shorts. "Race you, Neesh!" they say as their feet splat in the little puddles of water on the changing-room floor.

"No thanks!" I call back. "I'll follow you out. I don't want to slip!" I take a deep breath and walk out of the changing room to the poolside.

It's so loud out here! A big dome encases the swimming area and the sounds of voices, water splashing and music echo around me. The pool is huge and it's not a regular rectangle-shaped pool, but more like a big indoor lake. It's got slides, a jacuzzi, a lazy river that goes outside and a wave machine!

Mum's standing poolside, arranging our towels on loungers.

"Where's Dad?" I ask.

"Oh, he's here somewhere. You know him, he'll be straight in the jacuzzi," says Mum.

I see Milo and Manny taking turns to dive into the water. The lifeguard blows his whistle at them and points to the *NO DIVING* sign. They both mouth, "Sorry," and come over to us sheepishly.

Just then Granny Jas pops up in the water in front of us. She's wearing an all-in-one swimsuit with long legs and arms on it. She's also got goggles on. She looks like a deep-sea diver!

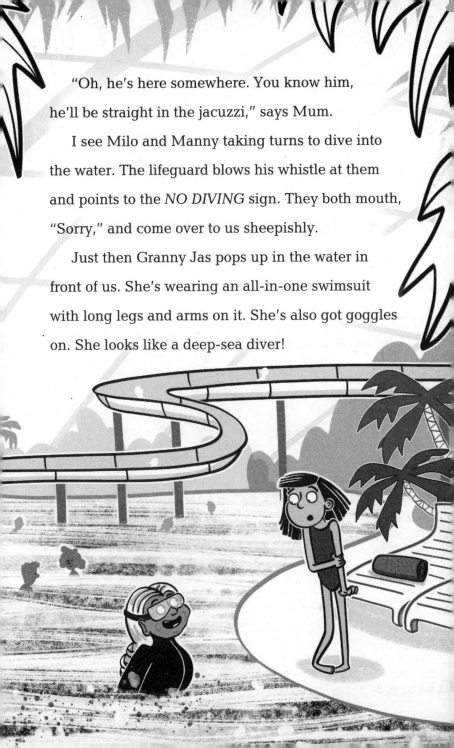

"Come on, slowcoaches, the water is lovely and warm," she says.

"Umm...I might in a bit," I say.

"I'll look after you, beta," Granny offers. "No need to worry, the water isn't very deep."

I look at her sceptically. "**Are you sure?**"

"Well, my feet touch the floor if I stand up!" She grins.

Just then Dad comes splashing past. "This is great!" he says. "Although Tony was right behind me – I don't know where he went. You okay, Anni?" he asks.

"Yeah, I'm okay, Dad," I say. I sit down on the side of the pool and dip my feet in the water. Granny was right, it is warm.

Uncle Tony comes wading over then too. "Bindi got chatting to one of the lifeguards and now they're talking about some film they both love," he tells us. "She was meant to go on the big slide with me. So who's coming now?"

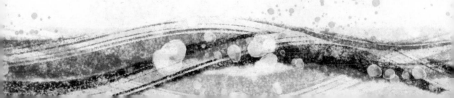

I shake my head, but right on cue Manny and Milo pop up and say, "We are, we are!"

"You could give it a try, Anni. I'd be right there with you," Dad says. "It's all very safe, you know."

Just then Dillon swims up to us. How does he do that? He's always everywhere we are!

"Hey, guys!" he says cheerfully. "Not coming in? I'll race you – I bet I can get to that end of the pool first."

"I'm not racing you," I say. "And you should be careful – the wave machine is that end and the sign says that the waves can get pretty big and strong."

"**Boring!** I'm the best swimmer in my school," Dillon brags and paddles off in the direction of the waves.

"He's such a **silly** boy," Granny comments.

"Well, are we going on this slide or not, family?"

Dad, Uncle Tony, Granny, Manny and Milo all swim off towards the steps for the big water slide.

I look around. There are a few members of the entertainment team doing a water aerobics session to music with some guests at the shallow end of the pool. There's a group of kids throwing a beach ball to each other and a man trying to swim lengths even though there's no space to do that and he keeps bumping into people.

Suddenly I hear a shout. I look over to where it's coming from. I can't see anyone, but I spot a hand splashing about in the waves. Is that Dillon? He's thrashing around. He's in **trouble**. I look around frantically for a lifeguard, but she's not in her chair by the poolside.

"Mum, look, that boy is in trouble!" I shout, pointing. "I can't see the lifeguard, Mum!"

Mum suddenly springs into action – I've never

seen her move so fast! She dives right in and swims over to a flapping Dillon, wrapping one arm round his chest. Then she uses her free arm to swim to the side of the pool, all the while dragging Dillon with her. The lifeguard has jumped in now too and helps her. They get him out of the water and wrap a towel round him.

"You're lucky this lady was here to help. You shouldn't go in the wave machine area if you're not a strong swimmer. Be more careful, okay? The signs are there for a reason," the lifeguard tells him. Dillon nods sheepishly.

Mum goes to get Dillon a warm drink and to find Dillon's parents. I sit on the chair next to him.

"You okay?" I ask.

"Yeah, I'm okay. You can laugh at me if you want," he replies.

"You don't need to show off for people to be your friend, you know," I say.

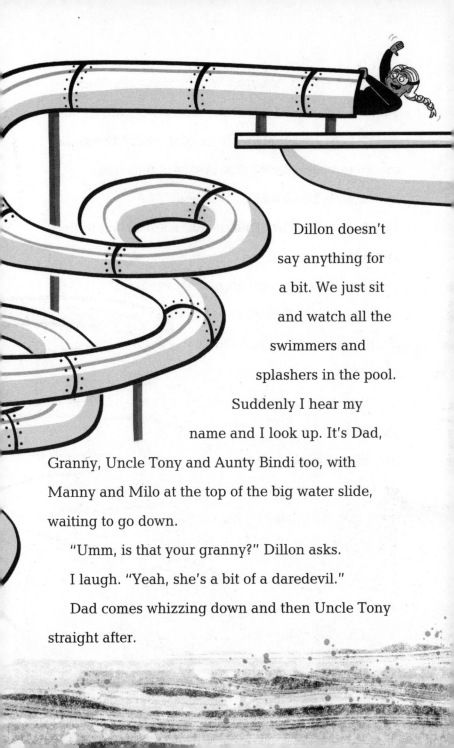

Dillon doesn't say anything for a bit. We just sit and watch all the swimmers and splashers in the pool. Suddenly I hear my name and I look up. It's Dad, Granny, Uncle Tony and Aunty Bindi too, with Manny and Milo at the top of the big water slide, waiting to go down.

"Umm, is that your granny?" Dillon asks.

I laugh. "Yeah, she's a bit of a daredevil."

Dad comes whizzing down and then Uncle Tony straight after.

"Your grown-ups are so cool," Dillon says. "My parents never do fun stuff with me."

"Where are they?" I ask.

"Somewhere here, probably with those other grown-ups they made friends with. They tell me to just go off and make friends. But it's not that easy, you know?"

I nod. "I'm **lucky**, I suppose – although it doesn't always feel like that when your whole family goes everywhere with you." I laugh.

"I guess." Dillon laughs too. "So, how's your break been so far? I mean, apart from me bugging you?"

"Well, we've been trying to prove that Cleo didn't destroy Delilah. But whenever we think we're getting somewhere, we hit another problem."

"Like what?" Dillon asks.

I stop a second. "Can I trust you? This is important stuff, Dillon, Cleo's job is at risk."

Dillon leans forward. "Look, I know we didn't get

off to the best start and I joke around a lot, but I do get it – this is **serious**. You can trust me."

I think about what Mindy said before, about Dillon wanting a friend. I guess it wouldn't hurt to give him a chance.

"Okay, I'll tell you, but I mean it about this being important, Dillon. If you want to be friends with us, trust is really important, okay?"

Dillon nods and I continue. "So we thought the person who really vandalized Delilah might have been Bobby, another member of the entertainment team. But he's too short to have reached the paint we think was used and he's afraid of heights. Then I saw Jamil, who is also a member of the team and he uses stilts – so that could possibly be the height thing sorted. But now I need to test something out. Will you help me?"

"Sure, what do we need to do?" Dillon asks.

"We need to see how long it would take to get from the craft supply shed to Delilah. We saw

Delilah at 8.30 a.m. and she was fine. But by 9.25 she'd been vandalized. We saw Jamil over by the outdoor exercise equipment on his stilts around 8.20. In order to have vandalized Delilah, he would have had to go to the shed, get the paint, make his way to Delilah, commit the crime, then take the wing he ripped off and hide it somewhere, and be back by the activities tent for his stilt-walking session at 8.50 a.m. – I checked the schedule."

"How do you know he didn't already have the paint?" Dillon asks.

"Well, we're assuming. He wasn't carrying anything when we saw him. The tubes of paint are pretty big, too big for a pocket so I'm guessing he still had to pick it up before going to Delilah. We also need to see if the jacket that had the paint on it would fit him – that's our key piece of evidence," I explain.

"Okay, makes sense, but if you're saying he had to have been able to do all that in half an hour, he'd need to have been **pretty quick** and I don't think he's that fast on his stilts, Anisha. I saw him on them earlier today and he was quite slow."

"Okay, well, then we definitely need to test out the theory," I say.

Just then we see Granny is at the front of the queue for the water slide again. She gives us a wave and then disappears from view as she sits down to start the slide. I hear her **whooping** through the tunnel and then we see her whizzing past in the clear see-through bit. She lands with a splash at the bottom and almost knocks Dad flying.

"You're supposed to move away from the landing area, Dad!" I call out.

I see Aunty Bindi join them and she follows, squealing more loudly than anyone else. She comes flying out of the tunnel and lands neatly in Uncle Tony's arms. He looks more surprised than anyone and promptly drops her in the water.

"Oops, sweetums, I'm so sorry!" he says, trying to pull up Aunty Bindi as she gasps and splutters.

Milo and Manny come down then too, whooping and laughing as they go shooting along the slide.

"That was the absolute best thing **EVER!**" Manny says. "Let's do it again!"

Dillon laughs. "Do you think they'd mind if I went too?"

"Ask them!" I say encouragingly, giving Manny and Milo a thumbs up as Dillon jumps in the pool and paddles towards them.

Dillon turns to me in the water. "Oh, by the way, I won't prank you any more. I guess it was a little annoying. Maybe we could be friends?"

"Agreed," I say, smiling. "Friends. Now let's solve this mystery!"

CHAPTER THIRTEEN

STILTS AND SKATES

Once everyone has had enough of the slides and splashing about, we get out of the pool and dry off. Granny Jas decides to stay in a bit longer, while the other grown-ups go to the cafe to get tea and cake.

Milo looks at me longingly at the mention of cake. "Have we got time, Neesh? We could take it with us!"

"Fine," I laugh. "But we can't waste any more time today. I feel like we're getting closer to finding out the truth."

A little while later, with tummies full of doughnut and mouths coated in sugar, we go back to the activities tent to find some stilts. Jamil is there, teaching some little kids how to walk on baby stilts, which are basically upside-down buckets on a long string.

We go over. "Can we try?" I ask, trying not to sound too high-pitched.

Jamil barely looks at us. "Yeah, help yourselves, stilts and helmets are there. Best put on knee pads as well, just in case. Don't wander off too far either."

There are only two pairs of stilts left, so Dillon and I decide to try them while Milo and Manny watch and shout advice at us. We run to where we saw Jamil yesterday morning and sit on the wall nearby to put our stilts on.

"Make sure you use both Velcro straps, Dillon, and wrap them tight," I say. "You do not want to come off these things and end up in a tree!"

"Have you done this before, Anisha?" Dillon asks.

"Well, no, but it seems sensible to do the straps properly, don't you think? I'm a bit cautious since Mindy got hurt!" I reply.

We both attach our stilts and then it's time to stand up. Milo helps me and Manny helps Dillon.

We're standing!

"Woah, this feels weird!" Dillon says as he wobbles next to me.

I sway a bit. "I feel like I'm really high up – maybe this wasn't a good idea!"

"You're up there now, might as well see if you can walk on them and test out your theory!" Milo shouts up.

"Okay," I say, unsure. "Dillon, let's take it slowly and see if we can get to that tree over there to start with."

So we head off gingerly. Dillon gets quite competitive and almost goes flying. I take my time and after a bit I think I'm getting the hang of this.

"Okay, let's see how long it takes on stilts to get from here to the supply shed and then to Delilah and back to the activities tent," I say.

"You sure you can make it?" Dillon asks. "You look kind of shaky," he says as he almost loses his balance again.

"No more shaky than you!" I say, feeling brave. "I bet I can get there before you and without falling over!"

"Umm, Neesh, take it easy, we're already a Mindy down, we can't be a Neesh down as well. There'll be no one left to solve the case!" Milo warns.

"I'll be fine!" I say a little too brightly and with that we set off.

We **wobble** and **wibble** our way to the supplies shed. Luckily there's no one around to see us almost fall into it! Then we shuffle and sway over to Delilah, who still looks **dreadful**, poor thing. From there we **waddle** to the activities tent. In the end we give up on who can get there first – it feels more important to get there standing up without planting my face in the floor!

"How was that?" I huff as we both plonk ourselves on a bench with our legs and stilts outstretched. "How long did it take us?"

Manny looks at the timer on his phone. "Umm, not great, it took fifty-five minutes! Manny and I played about 500 games of **I SPY** while we were waiting for you!"

"What? It can't have been that long!" I say. "Are you sure?"

"Yeah, look!" Manny says, holding out the phone to show us.

"But Jamil is more experienced than you guys, maybe he did it faster?" Milo suggests.

"Not that much faster – remember, he's kind of slow on the stilts too," Dillon says.

"Okay, well, if he took the stilts off and did the whole thing on foot, he might have been able to run fast enough," I say.

"Yeah, but he would have had to take them with him or hide them and come back for them. Seems like a lot of hassle," Milo says.

"Plus I think it would still have taken too long. He only had a short amount of time – he was back at his stilt-walking workshop for 8.50 a.m. and he probably had to be there a few minutes early to get everything ready for that too," Dillon replies, as we both unstrap our own stilts. "It's too fiddly to do quickly," he adds as his Velcro gets stuck and Manny has to help yank it free.

"Okay, so we're back to where we started then." Milo shrugs.

"I feel like we have some of the pieces of the puzzle but they're not quite fitting together," I say. "Like, Bobby has access to the paint but couldn't reach it. Jamil could reach it but couldn't have got to Delilah in time." Just then a group of kids go past on roller skates. There are six of them being led by the roller-skating instructor, Rae.

"Remember yesterday we started out roller-skating," I murmur.

"Yeah, and then Mindy fell," Milo says.

"Yeah, but before that, the whole reason we decided to try the roller skating first was because of **Rae, the instructor**. When I mentioned to her that

Cleo had been fired for what happened to Delilah, she freaked out a bit. It was **weird**. Plus she's about the same size as Cleo so we thought the jacket might fit her. But then we forgot about her because we moved onto Bobby – and then Mindy sprained her ankle... But **what if** Rae *was* involved? On skates, she'd be able to whizz around the park in no time at all!"

Milo, Manny and Dillon all look at each other.

Dillon grins. "What are we waiting for then? Follow those skaters!"

CHAPTER FOURTEEN

INTO THE SHED!

The skaters are fast, so we have to jog behind them at a distance to keep up. Thankfully this part of the park is quite busy, so we don't look suspicious. After a little while, Rae stops and the skating session appears to be over. The four of us stop too and pretend to do warm-down stretches on the grass. I realize we're right by another equipment shed. Rae instructs the kids to leave their skates by the shed door. When one of the boys offers to help put them away, she shakes her head and dismisses the group. She waits for them to leave and looks around. Then she pulls a key out of her pocket, opens the shed door and goes inside.

"She didn't take the skates with her, that's weird," Milo says.

Manny pulls out his binoculars. "I can't see what she's doing, the window is blacked out."

A moment later Rae comes out of the shed, throws the kids' skates inside and pulls the door shut behind her. She looks around again and then starts to skate off.

"Can I borrow those binoculars a second?" I whisper.

Manny passes them to me and I use them to look closely at Rae's feet. She's got something yellow stuck to the bottom of one of her roller skates. But as she moves off it comes loose and falls to the floor. We wait for her to disappear out of sight, and then I run over.

I kneel down and pick up the yellow thing. It's a scrap of fabric, like the stuff Delilah's wings are made of, and it's covered in yellow paint. I turn to the others and call them over.

"We need to get inside that shed. Look what I found – this was on Rae's skate and it looks like it came off Delilah."

"**Woah**, okay, you go in with Milo and we'll stay out here as lookouts," Manny says. "I'll radio you if anyone comes, okay?"

"Okay, let's go," I say.

Manny and Dillon go to sit at a nearby outdoor chess table, as if they're just having a game.

Milo and I approach the shed carefully and I push the door. **It's open!**

"Why didn't she lock it?" Milo wonders.

"She did look distracted, maybe she forgot,"

I say. "Now let's see, that piece of fabric must have got stuck to her skate in here, because I only noticed it after she came out of the shed."

We poke around, but there's not much in here apart from a few boxes, the pile of roller skates and some boards leaning against a shelf.

"What's behind there?" I point. "Help me move these boards, Milo. They're a bit heavy."

Milo kneels down and grabs hold of the bottom of the boards while I get the other end. We have to wiggle them a bit to get them out, but then we lift them away and place them to the side, revealing some shopping bags filled with craft stuff. When we move those out of the way too, behind them is something big and bulky wrapped in a sheet. I peel the material back...

There it is! **Delilah's wing!**

"We found it!" Milo shouts.

"I can't believe it," I say. I feel so happy – I can't wait to show Cleo. "Wait – that's weird though."

"What is?"

"Look at this part of the wing – there's white paint on the fabric, but you can tell the yellow splashes are underneath. Why would she put white paint on it? She couldn't be trying to **fix** it, could she?"

"That wouldn't make sense though, would it? Why break it and then try to fix it?"

"Unless it was an accident," I say, an idea starting to form in my mind. But before I can finish the thought, my radio crackles and Manny's voice comes over.

"*Psst, bluebird calling yellow duck.*"

"Huh?" I say into the radio. "Who's bluebird?"

"*It's Manny – bluebird is my code name and yours is yellow duck,*" Manny whispers.

"Oh, okay. Might have been helpful to know that before. Anyway, what's up? We've found Delilah's wing!"

"*Amazing! Well, you need to come out here and listen to this right away,*" Manny says.

"*You really do,*" Dillon adds in the background.

"Okay, we're coming," I answer.

"*Bluebird, over and out,*" Manny says.

"Okay, bye," I say.

"*No, not like that, you're supposed to say 'Yellow duck, over and out',*" Manny complains.

We wrap the wing back up in the sheet and carry it outside, then run with it over to Manny and Dillon.

"What was so urgent?" I ask.

Manny grins. "So I was twizzling the knobs on the radio to try and get a better signal and I accidentally joined the frequency that some of the entertainment team use..."

"Oh, okay, and?" I ask.

"Well, when I realized who was talking on there, I started recording using my phone. Listen." Manny puts his phone down on the chess table and presses play.

"Did you do it, Rae?" a voice asks.

"Yeah, Bobby, I tried, but I need more time," Rae answers.

"We don't have more time. We need to meet by Delilah at 10 p.m. tonight." I'm pretty sure that's Jamil.

"And what about the video? The deadline is midnight tonight," Bobby says.

"We have to forget about that now. We just have to concentrate on Delilah," Rae answers firmly.

Manny pauses the recording. "You know what this means, right?"

"It's all three of them!" I say. "**They ALL did it!**"

CHAPTER FIFTEEN

FIGURING IT OUT

"It all makes sense now," I say. "They all had a part to play in what happened. So let's break it down. At 8.20 we saw Jamil, right? He goes to the supply shed in his stilts, reaches down the paint and gives it to Bobby. He then goes to his stilt-walking workshop for 8.50. In the meantime, Bobby passes the paint to Rae, who, as we know, is super-fast on her roller skates. She whizzes over to Delilah and vandalizes her, grabs the wing and hides it, before the damage is found at 9.25. Maybe she passes the brush she used wrapped in a paint-stained rag to Bobby to hide, but we saw him with it before he had the chance. But I'm still wondering why? Why did they do it?"

"Why?" Milo asks. "Well, maybe they thought it would be funny."

"What, like a prank?" I ask.

Dillon frowns. "Yes, exactly like a prank, **a prize-winning prank!** Remember, I was pranking everyone when we first met, but I never told you why."

"Why?" I ask.

"I have one word for you that basically solves this case," Dillon says proudly. "**PRANKFEST!**"

"What's **Prankfest**?" we all ask.

"It's the ultimate online festival of pranking. You play your best pranks and then upload a video or pictures. The best ones win prizes! I've never won and I thought it would be cool if I did." Dillon shrugs.

"It sounds gross if they're encouraging people to vandalize stuff that doesn't belong to them," I say.

Dillon sits up straighter. "No, Anisha, that's one of the rules of **Prankfest**: no vandalism, no destroying other people's property or deliberately hurting anyone."

"Hmm, well, if that's what Rae and the others were trying to do then I don't think they understood the part about no vandalism," I say, pointing at the wing under the chess table.

"But it does make sense, right?" Dillon says. "And on that recording you heard them talk about a deadline. Well, the deadline for **Prankfest** is midnight tonight. I think that's why they did it, but maybe they didn't mean for it to go so far."

"Are you sticking up for them?" Milo asks.

"No, I just know sometimes I do silly pranks and it's meant to be funny but then occasionally it accidentally goes wrong."

"Like Mindy getting hurt," Manny points out.

Dillon looks sheepish. "Yeah, I heard afterwards about her fall. I am sorry I caused that, dude. I really

wasn't trying to hurt anyone – and maybe, just maybe, Rae and the others weren't either."

Manny shrugs. "He could have a point, Anisha."

"Okay, but how do we find out what the truth is?" Milo asks.

"We go to their meeting at 10 p.m.," I say.

"Are you kidding? Our parents won't let us out at that time!" Manny laughs.

"What if you said you were sleeping round at my lodge?" Dillon asks. "It's only next door to your lodge so your parents won't worry and my parents won't even realize we're gone. We'll be back before anyone notices."

"That's actually a good idea," I say. "Right, this is the plan then. We'll take this wing to Cleo's lodge, so we can check the new wing Cleo and Mindy have been working on matches up for size. Then tonight we'll stake out the meeting point by Delilah and hopefully catch Bobby, Jamil and Rae **in the act**."

"Do you think they're going to do more damage?" Milo asks, looking worried as we pick up the wrapped wing and start walking.

"I don't know, but if they are planning to, we'll be there to stop them. And we need to make them own up to Tom, because Cleo has got the blame and that's not right."

"Yeah, like, how can they be okay with that?" Milo says. "I feel bad if I even think I've upset someone by accident. If I made someone lose their job, I wouldn't be able to keep it secret, I'd have to tell on myself!"

It doesn't take long to get to Cleo's lodge and we burst in, all talking at once.

"Hang on, one at a time!" Cleo says, standing up.

So I tell Mindy and Cleo what we've learned, show them the wing we found and then I explain what our plan is.

"All this was because of a prank?" Cleo says in disbelief.

"We think so, but we're going to put it right,"
I say. "We'll get your job back, Cleo."

"So you want to ambush them when they meet at
10 p.m.? When it's dark?" Mindy asks.

"**YESSS!**" Manny jumps up.

"Why are you so excited about it being dark?"
Mindy asks.

"Because it means you finally have to listen to
me. I've got survival skills, remember, and I've had
training for exactly this sort of situation." He stands
with his legs apart and puts
his hands on his hips.

**"Manny Singh,
Survival Expert**
at your service."

"Survival
expert?" Mindy
snorts. "And
training? You've
watched some episodes

of a documentary with that mountain-climbing guy, that's your training?"

"**ALL** the episodes, and yes, I know everything I need to know. More than you, anyway. I'm not the one who fell in a bush, after all," Manny says, sticking his tongue out at his sister.

Mindy huffs and folds her arms. "Whatever. I'm not coming to rescue you when you get scared."

"I just thought of something really cool," Dillon interrupts.

"What?" I ask.

"I could film us catching them in the act. I even have an idea about how we can get them to confess. It'll be the ultimate prank! I just need a megaphone and one of those duck whistles – you know, it's like a normal whistle but it makes a quacking sound."

"Oh wow, this is going to be a night to remember!" Milo grins.

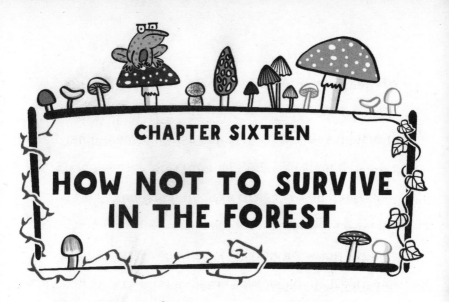

CHAPTER SIXTEEN

HOW NOT TO SURVIVE IN THE FOREST

Manny, Milo, Dillon and I go to gather some supplies for our **stakeout** later and hide them near Delilah. By the time we're all done, it's dinner time. We head back to collect Mindy, leaving Cleo to put the last finishing touches to the wing, and race back to our lodge. Dillon runs into his – we've agreed to go over there in a little while.

Over dinner we tell our grown-ups about staying over at Dillon's. Luckily Mum, Dad, Uncle Tony and Aunty Bindi are fine about us sleeping next door. Turns out they met Dillon's parents at a cheese-tasting class earlier, so they're all friends now.

Granny, however, takes a bit more convincing.

"I thought you didn't like this boy – wasn't he annoying you yesterday?" she asks, narrowing her eyes so it feels like she's looking right into my brain.

"Umm, he's not **that** annoying any more," I say. "Plus you always say people deserve a second chance, right? Anyway, I've had enough to eat. I'm quite tired, actually. We should get round to Dillon's early so we can all get a good sleep before the party tomorrow. Better go and pack my toothbrush!" I say and quickly run up the stairs.

"Yeah, me too!" says Mindy, hobbling up behind me.

"And us!" shout Milo and Manny.

From the landing I hear Granny say to Dad, "They're up to something, I can feel it in my bones."

"No, they're just excited," Dad replies.

"Yeah, it's sweet. When Mindy hurt herself I thought that was the holiday ruined, but they all seem really happy today," Bindi says.

"Yeah, and if they're having a sleepover why don't we go down to watch the entertainment this evening? I hear they've got a flame-throwing act," Uncle Tony says.

"Maybe they'll let me have a try," Granny replies.

"Er, no, Mum!" Dad starts.

"How do you know? I might be a natural at it!" Granny says.

That's good, they'll all be out of the way this evening now. I nod at the others and we go into our rooms to get our stuff together.

A little while later we go round to Dillon's with a bag of our stuff. His parents are sitting out on their patio at the back of the lodge with another couple. They all give us a wave as we go past them and up the stairs to Dillon's room. It's still only 7 p.m., so we chill out for a bit. Manny insists on teaching us all survival tips from his favourite expert, like how to treat a poisonous **scorpion sting** and what to do if you are confronted by a **wild bear** in the forest. I'm not sure either of those things are likely to happen here, but Manny is very enthusiastic about it.

We all get dressed in black or green clothes, because Manny told us they're the best colours for blending in. Milo has had to borrow something of Manny's, because all his T-shirts are bright colours.

"My hair! It's going to stand out even in the dark," Milo complains, patting his ginger hair down.

"Never fear, Manny Singh, Survival Expert is here," Manny says, pulling out a black balaclava.

"Are you a survival expert or a bank robber?" Mindy asks.

"It's good for camouflaging. I've got green face

paint in my backpack if you want some," Manny offers.

"That's okay, I think we're good," Mindy giggles.

Soon it's 9 p.m. – time to leave. We want to make sure we have plenty of time to set up our trap and be ready when Rae, Jamil and Bobby get there. Dillon creeps downstairs to check on his parents. They're still sitting outside on the candlelit porch, laughing and chatting with their guests, so we can **sneak out** without them seeing. Grown-ups are so easy to get past when they're distracted! Dillon says his parents can talk for England and he reckons they'll be out there till late too. We'll be back before they even notice.

We leave the lodge excitedly and we're feeling really pleased with ourselves when we walk straight into...**GRANNY JAS!**

"And where do you think you are all going?" she asks with her hands on her hips.

"Oh, Granny, you scared us! What are you doing lurking in the dark like that?"

Granny snorts. "I know my Anni and you had a shifty look about you earlier like you're up to something. Granny knows when a plan is afoot. I had a feeling this whole sleepover thing was a big excuse so you could sneak out. Now spill the lentils!"

"We know who vandalized Delilah and we're going to set a trap for them!" Dillon says too loudly.

"Dillon!" I hiss. "We don't want the whole forest to know. Not yet anyway."

Dillon goes a bit pink. "Oops, yeah, sorry!" he says, and quickly steps back.

Granny punches the air and does a little jump. "I knew it! Who did it? Tell me, I'll sort them out!"

I look at the others – we'll have to tell Granny the truth. "We think some of the members of the entertainment team did it for a prank," I say.

"A **prank**? What is that, like a joke? Because it wasn't funny," Granny huffs.

"Well, we're going to make them confess and get Cleo's job back," Mindy says.

"Okay, so tell me, what's the plan?" Granny asks, linking arms with me as we walk.

"You're coming with us?" I ask.

"Beta, you are **NOT** wandering around by yourselves in the forest in the dark. Either I come with you or I get your parents."

"Okay, okay!" I say, raising my hands. "You got us, Granny, you can come with us."

"Plus," says Granny, "I have snacks!" And she pulls out a little lunch bag.

She's got a ziplock bag filled with nuts and chevda*
and my favourites, chocolate digestive biscuits.

"Oh, I don't think we'll have time for that," I say.

"Nonsense! You can't fight crime on an empty
stomach and you hardly ate anything at dinner,"
Granny scolds.

"She's right and you'll be starving later," Mindy
tells me.

"Yeah, and we don't want your rumbling tummy
giving us away when we're meant to be hiding out,"
Manny laughs.

"I hate when that happens in class and everyone
looks at you!" Mindy says.

"Yeah, me too," Milo agrees.

"Alright, I'll eat something while we walk," I say
taking a biscuit, secretly glad that Granny is here
with us.

It's a dark cool night and only the lamps on the
path give us any light. It feels like it gets darker the

★☆☆🌟★🌠☆🌟★🌟★★🌠☆★🌠☆🌠★🌟★☆🌠★☆★🌠🌟★

* Chevda is a snack mix made up of spicy dried ingredients, like
fried lentils, peanuts, chickpeas, puffed rice, fried onion and
curry leaves. It doesn't sound that nice when I describe it but
it's yummy although I usually get carried away, eat too much
and then get a tummy ache.

further we walk, so Manny uses the light from his phone to guide us. We huddle together and walk towards the main building and Delilah. None of us have any idea what will happen when our suspects arrive but we're on a mission and we're going to get the truth **no matter what**.

When we get there it's hard to see anything apart from the uplighting in Delilah's base. It makes her look kind of sinister!

"**Boo!**" A dark figure leaps out from behind Delilah and makes us all jump!

"**Arrgh!** Don't come any closer!" Granny Jas warns, pulling out a rolling pin from inside her cardigan.

"Granny, why have you got that with you?" I whisper.

"Well, you never know what danger

might be lurking. And look, aren't you glad I have it now?" Granny points it at the dark hooded figure.

They step into the light. "It's only me!"

It's Cleo! I'm so relieved!

"Cleo, you scared us!" Mindy laughs.

"Sorry, I was only playing about – but I've got to say your granny kind of scared me too," Cleo chuckles.

"Yeah, Granny doesn't mess around," I say. "Right, let's set up our trap. We haven't got long."

Manny pulls out our bag of supplies, which he and Milo hid here earlier. We open it up and take out the following items:

☆ **Torch**

● **Duck whistle**

★ **Net**

✩ **Infrared binoculars**

● **Megaphone**

✳ **Strong string**

Manny and Dillon set up
the net and Manny positions himself high up
in a tree behind Delilah.

"Try it now," I say.

Manny does a duck call through the whistle.
It sounds quite realistic. He does it again. Another
duck calls out a reply from somewhere deep in the
forest.

"Sorry to disturb you!" Milo whisper-shouts to
the real duck.

"Sounds pretty convincing," I say.

"Now, what is going to happen? Manny will
pretend to be the duck and scare them into telling
the truth?" Granny asks.

"Yeah, and I'm going to film the whole thing
for **Prankfest!**" Dillon grins, pulling out his
camera.

"Is this going to work?" Mindy asks, leaning
on Delilah's base to rest her injured ankle.

"I have no idea, but it's worth a try," I say.

Just then we
hear a twig crack
in the distance and then
muffled voices. It must be them!

"Quick, places, everyone!" I say.

Manny stays where he is in the tree. Milo
hides behind it. Mindy, Cleo and I crawl
behind a nearby bush. Granny Jas hides
behind Delilah and Dillon positions himself
under a bench across from Delilah so he can
film. It suddenly occurs to me that this is
the second time this trip that I've
ended up in a bush. Well, Dad
wanted us to get back to nature!

The voices get nearer, Mindy
grabs my arm and we sit there,
frozen, waiting for something to happen.
I peer carefully round the side of the bush.
It's them – Rae, Bobby and Jamil. This is it!

CHAPTER SEVENTEEN

CAUGHT!

I hold my breath as we wait for them to say something. It feels like for ever before Rae speaks.

"Right, let's get this thing done and get out of here," she says.

Just then Manny quacks into action. He does a short burst on the duck whistle, which makes all three of them jump.

"**WHAT** was that?" Jamil trembles.

"I think it came from her." Bobby points to Delilah.

"Don't be silly, it's just a statue," Rae says.

Manny blows the duck whistle again, but this time uses his voice to make it sound like a word. **"GUILTY!"**

For a second even I believe Delilah is talking – Manny is really convincing!

Rae stares at Delilah. "Did she just say 'guilty'?"

Bobby looks horrified. "No, she couldn't. She's a statue. She can't talk. **CAN SHE?**"

Jamil hops from one foot to the other. "I think it's a sign. She knows what we did."

Rae scoffs but she looks unsure too. Manny does it again and this time he uses the string we attached to Delilah's unbroken wing to lift it and flap it up and down, so it really does look like Delilah has come to life! I hope Dillon's getting all this on film.

"Did you see that?" Rae shrieks. "She **IS** alive. I don't know how, but she is and she knows what we did. It doesn't matter that it was an accident! Look, let's just do what we came to do and get out of here."

Just then Milo pulls a cord and drops the net on them and they're trapped.

"Oi!" someone shouts.

"Stay still!" another one of them yells.

"You're pulling me down, hang on, we just need some scissors."

I jump out from where I've been hiding and shine the torchlight in their faces. "You've been caught – you might as well confess. We know you vandalized Delilah, even it was just for some silly prank. She's a poor defenceless duck and you maimed her!"

"Yeah, you maimed her, you monsters!" Milo yells as he steps out from the shadows too.

"Yeah, prank's on you!" shouts Dillon as he emerges from under the bench, still filming.

"We don't know what you mean and can you get that light out of my face!" Rae screams at us.

"You've been caught, just admit it – you came back to finish Delilah off but we stopped you," Mindy says.

"You're all wrong and if you don't let us out of here, I'm going to call security," Rae warns.

"But then how do we explain what we're doing here, Rae? Delilah knows, remember," a **scared-sounding** Jamil adds.

"Shut up!" Rae hisses.

"Look, we didn't mean for it to go this far," Bobby interrupts.

Rae glares at him. "Not another word!"

"But they obviously know we had something to do with it. If they call Tom, we'll have to fess up anyway," Jamil says.

"If you agree to tell us what happened, we'll get you out of that net," I offer.

Rae moans. "Oh, alright then. I should have known these two would drop us right in it anyway."

As we help them out of the net, Rae looks **guiltily** at Cleo. "We never meant for you to get in trouble. How was I supposed to know you'd pick up my stained jacket and put it on?"

"You could have owned up right there and then,"

Cleo says. "But you didn't, you just let me take the blame. I've lost my job."

"We were scared. We saw you get fired and we were worried that would happen to us," Rae replies. "We thought if we could fix Delilah, we could put things right."

"Well, I guess it'll be us losing our jobs after all," Jamil grumbles.

"Not necessarily," I say. "If you admit what you did, you might not get fired. You said before that it was an accident. We thought it was a prank."

"Yeah, that's exactly it – it was both, kind of," Bobby says. "It started with **Prankfest**, the online pranking competition. It was just meant to be a bit of fun."

"You convinced us we'd win a prize – you said we might win five hundred pounds!" Rae complains.

"I hardly forced you to take part!" Bobby fires back.

"Yeah, but it wasn't meant to be that **extreme**.

The original prank was that we were going to dress ourselves as ducks. We were even going to paint our faces and arms and legs yellow. We made duck masks and everything," Jamil explains.

"Wow, so what were you going to do once you were dressed as ducks?" I ask.

"We were going to run round the park quacking at guests and just being a bit silly. We were going to film it and enter it into **Prankfest**," says Bobby.

"But then how did you go from that to pulling off Delilah's whole wing and splattering yellow paint all over her?" I ask.

Rae frowns. "It would have been fine. I wanted to film a little intro to the prank by Delilah to explain why we were dressing as ducks. I put the paint tube next to Delilah on her base just for a moment. But then Bobby was goofing about behind me and he tripped and pushed into me! I fell forward onto the tube, which squirted paint **everywhere**, and in trying to steady myself I reached out and grabbed onto Delilah's wing, which then came off in my hand!"

"You expect us to believe that?" Granny says, raising an eyebrow.

"Yes, it's all true! We have the whole thing recorded to prove it," Bobby says. "I did bump into her and it did happen exactly like Rae said. We panicked, took the wing with us and ran."

Rae looks down at her feet. "I saw I had paint on my jacket and I just dumped it without thinking. I never imagined someone else would pick it up and then get the blame! I'm **really** sorry, Cleo," she finishes.

Jamil steps forward. "After Cleo was fired, we tried to mend the wing, but the paint was all smudged and we had no idea how to fix the wing back on without anyone seeing. Bobby had even found a tool and a reel of wire to help us reattach it."

"Were you carrying it wrapped up in a yellow-paint-stained rag yesterday by any chance?" I ask.

"Yeah, how did you know?" Bobby asks. "It would have worked too, but then the wing went missing and it's just been a **nightmare!**"

"Yeah, I had only just checked on it a little earlier this afternoon, but when I came back an hour later it was gone! Wait, was that you lot?"

Granny Jas says, "**Bete**, why didn't you just own up? Honesty is the best policy, no?"

Rae sniffs. "We know that, but we were scared of losing our jobs over a silly prank that went wrong. And we really have been trying to put things right."

"Well, we might be able to help with the fixing, but you still have to own up so that Tom knows it wasn't Cleo," I say.

"Aww, man, really?" Bobby groans. "Can't we just fix it? And then everyone will think it's a miracle and be all happy and maybe Cleo will get her job back anyway." He grins uncertainly.

Granny waggles her finger at him. "Young man, there will be **none of that!** Come on, we'll walk you to the office to make sure you tell the truth."

Once again, I'm really glad my Granny Jas is here.

I can't believe we did it. **We solved the mystery!**

CHAPTER EIGHTEEN

MISSION DUCK

We go with Bobby, Jamil and Rae to find Tom, who is out patrolling the grounds with Mr Judge in case there's any more vandalism. We leave them explaining and Tom not looking very happy at all.

Cleo hugs us all. "You are **amazing**, I don't know how to thank you for everything," she says.

"It's not over yet," I say. "We still have to fix Delilah's wing back on in time for the party. We'll see you bright and early tomorrow back here."

Granny gets us all to link arms and we head back to our lodge.

"I'm so tired!" Milo yawns. "What time is it?"

"11.30 p.m., way past your bedtime, Milo Moon

– and all of our bedtimes." Mindy smiles.

"I'm kind of hungry though," Manny says.

"I think I can rustle something up," Granny Jas says, even though she's yawning too.

"Don't do it, Manny! You remember what happened that time you ate cheese right before bed?" Mindy warns.

"Oh yeah… You know what? I'm not that hungry," Manny replies.

"What happened last time?" I ask.

"Let's just say Manny did not sleep well that night. He kept shouting out about a giant onion ring chasing him," Mindy answers.

We get back to the lodge and say goodnight to each other. I can't believe what a long day it's been. I'm so tired!

Granny stops me at the bottom of the stairs and whispers, "I'm so proud of you, **beta**. You always stand up for those who need help. Never change, okay?"

That night I dream about everything that's happened but all mixed up. I'm going down the big water slide wearing a duck head and weirdly Granny Jas has a duck body but her own Granny face! It's all very strange.

Surprisingly, I wake up feeling refreshed. We all jump up and get dressed quickly. We know we have a lot to do today. It's the day of Delilah's party!

"The party is at 1 p.m., right, Neesh?" Milo asks me.

"Yes, so we need to get the wing round to Delilah after breakfast," I reply.

Granny makes toast and eggs for everyone and we tuck in. Late night stakeouts make me hungry.

Mum, Dad, Aunty Bindi and Uncle Tony are all having a lie-in. We leave Granny to fill them in on everything and we head over to Cleo's. It's still only 8.30 in the morning, so we've got lots of time before the party. Last night we told Tom not to worry about Delilah and that we have it all in hand. Well, actually Milo said we have it all "under the wing", but Tom didn't look like he got the joke. It was late.

"Are you ready to see it?" Cleo asks us, smiling as she stands in front of the wing. "We did our best. I think it looks even better than before, personally."

Mindy stands next to her. "We worked so hard on this, I'm nervous for you to see it now!"

"Show us!" we all shout excitedly.

Mindy and Cleo part to reveal
the wing. It looks gorgeous.
They've replaced the paint-
stained strips of fabric with
new ones, all different
colours and patterns,
layers and layers of them.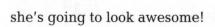
It's a rainbow wing now!
It doesn't even matter
that Delilah's wings
are not matching,
she's going to look awesome!

"Now we just have to attach it back onto
Delilah," Manny says.

"No problem, the maintenance team will have
some tools for that," Cleo replies. "I need help
carrying it there though."

So we all take an edge of the wing and together
we carry it outside and back through the forest to
Delilah. I swear she looks happy to see us, even

though she's a statue. Jo and the maintenance team come and slowly fix the wing back onto Delilah and before we know it, she's back to being her glorious ducky self.

"Selfie?" Cleo asks.

So we all gather round with big smiles and take a picture in front of Delilah – and if I didn't know better, I would say Delilah is smiling too!

"Right, do you all want to stick around and help with the party stuff?" Cleo asks us.

"Umm…we'd love to and we might come back in a bit to help, but there's an important job we have to do first, right, Milo?" I say. "The family of ducks still need our help."

Milo beams. "Yes, **Mission Duck** is a go."

"Wait, but you fixed the duck," Cleo says, pointing at Delilah.

"There's more than one duck that needs our help," Milo shouts as he runs back towards our lodge. We wave at Cleo and follow him.

When we get back to the lodge, all the grown-ups have finally got out of bed. Mum and Dad are sitting at the table, having some breakfast, while Aunty

Bindi is sitting on the sofa and Uncle Tony is washing up. Granny is doing her morning stretches.

"Everyone needs to help!" I say.

"Ooh, what with, **beta**?" Granny asks as she touches her toes.

"The ducks. We know where in the lake they need to get to and now we need to help them find their way there. We've got a plan," I explain.

So we gather up anything we can from the fridge and cupboard that ducks eat. Sweetcorn, lettuce, oats and peas. Milo pulls out the bag of seeds he bought from the gift shop too. We carefully lay a trail from the back patio doors through the lodge and out the front door.

"Aren't the ducks usually waddling about at the back of the lodge?" Manny says.

"They're probably out there now; we just need to call them," Milo says, like it's the most obvious thing ever.

He and Manny go out to the patio, leaving the

door open behind them. They start quacking and flapping their arms like they did the other day. Mindy and I can't help but laugh. Do they **really** think that's going to work? But then suddenly out of the forest comes the mama duck, followed closely by her ducklings. It worked! The ducks peck away at the trail of seeds and oats and other treats. Every so often they stop to gulp their food down and then off they go again.

Milo and Manny keep quacking and walk backwards through the patio doors and into the lodge.

"What now?" Manny asks in between quacks.

"We keep going," Milo answers. "Come on, everyone. Granny, can you and Aunty Bindi take up the back of the line and make sure we don't lose any ducklings?"

"I'll help, I suppose. As long as they don't hiss at me," Aunty Bindi says nervously, jumping a little way behind the ducks.

Granny Jas joins her and salutes Milo. "Lead on, Milo!"

Mum and Dad stand either side of the line of ducks and Mindy and I go up ahead of Manny and Milo. Manny gets out his phone and starts recording the whole thing as we walk.

"Neesh, can you stay a few steps ahead of us and look out for any park vehicles or bicycles," Milo asks.

"Don't worry, Milo, we've got this," I reassure him.

We must make a very strange sight as we emerge from the lodge. Mindy and I act as lookouts and as we pass Dillon's lodge, he waves at us. "Can I join in?" he asks.

"You can go at the end and help Granny and Aunty Bindi," I say.

So Dillon jumps down and joins the line. We make our way along the path, dropping treats as we go so the ducks have a trail to follow. As we walk, people from the other lodges come out and join the duck parade too. The ducks waddle along – they even look quite happy to have an audience.

Someone starts singing that song, "Five little ducks went swimming one day", and everyone joins in. By now there's about thirty people in the group following the little ducks. This is the most **bizarre** and **wonderful** thing I've ever been part of!

There's a bit of a scary moment when we cross paths with some children on a horse-riding lesson, but Milo stops the line and quacks something at the ducks and they seem to totally understand that we need to wait until the horses have passed.

Finally, we get to the lake
and Milo guides the ducks
down the muddy bank
and into the water. One
little duckling gets a bit
stuck and Milo picks her
up and places her gently
next to the mama duck. All
the ducks quack in appreciation
and then turn to swim away across the lake.

"I'm really going to miss them," Milo says.

"You did a really wonderful thing, Milo," Dad says.

"Yes, Milo, you're a wildlife hero!" adds Mum.

"That deserves an extra big plate of my samosas!"
says Granny Jas.

Milo beams. "Thanks for helping me, everyone.
I know I talk **A LOT** about animals, but they really are
important to me and to our environment."

"I know we joke about it, Milo, but honestly you
teach me so much. You should totally have a blog

page or something – I bet lots of people would love it," I say.

"We could all help!" Mindy says. "I'm quite good at building pages – I taught myself."

"I can film some footage," says Manny. "Plus we've got loads of pictures and video from this trip as a starter."

"Ooh, how exciting! I could do some presenting for you if you decide to do more videos," Aunty Bindi offers.

Uncle Tony puts his arm around her. "Well, sweetums, I think they might quite like to do that themselves."

"Oh, yes of course. But the offer's there if you need me," says Aunty Bindi. "I have many talents; I could be the face of wildlife in Britain today." She stares longingly into the distance.

"Ooh, is that the time?" Mum interrupts. "We'd better get back to the lodge to get ready for the party!"

Good subject change, Mum!

CHAPTER NINETEEN

DELILAH'S BIG CELEBRATION

After all the excitement of seeing the ducks off, we walk back to the lodge. It's almost 11.30, so we've got a little time to get changed for the big Delilah celebration at 1 p.m.

"What an eventful trip this has been," Dad says.

Milo nods. "I know, it's been wild. And now it's time to party! I hope they have some good food there."

"Hmm, yeah, hot dogs and burgers and chicken and potato salad." Manny rubs his tummy.

"I'm hoping there will be samosas and pakoras too – I gave the chef my special recipe!" Granny says. "You can't beat a good samosa and I did say your good deed with the ducks deserved an extra big plate of them, Milo!"

"Ooh, **yum!**" Milo says. "I love your samosas."

As we get ready I can't wait to get to the party and see Cleo. Hopefully everything has been sorted now and she's got her job back. I still can't believe everything we've done in the last few days. As a family, we've definitely made the most of our trip!

 Granny went down the zip wire and learned archery.

 Mum and Dad made brownies and did some pottery, which resulted in a very wonky pair of bowls.

 Aunty Bindi and Uncle Tony learned how to paint, model and use Segways.

I roller-skated badly.

 Mindy sprained an ankle and made a new wing for Delilah with Cleo.

 Manny taught us all important survival skills.

 I went on the zip wire and survived!

 Milo rescued a family of ducks.

 We all made a new friend in Dillon!

 We solved a mystery and saved Cleo's job.

Phew, that's a lot!

When everyone's ready we head back out again, all fresh and not smelling of ducks. We walk back to the main square to find it decorated with bunting, and Delilah covered over with a cloth. Jo from maintenance is there with Cleo.

"We thought you'd like to help unveil the new and improved Delilah." Cleo smiles.

Tom comes over then. "Ah, here she is, the best detective in all the forest!"

I blush. "Not really – and I had lots of help!"

"Don't be modest, you saved our celebration and Cleo's job. I've already apologized to Cleo, as has Mr Judge. We completely jumped to conclusions and it's only because you believed in finding out the truth that we're here celebrating today. I really mean it – thank you, Anisha. And as a token of our gratitude, we want to offer you and your family a weekend stay here whenever you'd next like to visit."

"**Wow!**" I say, looking at Mum and Dad, who are beaming. "I don't know what to say. Thank you. I'm just glad Delilah is fixed and Cleo gets to keep her job."

"And I can still afford to go to space camp," Cleo adds brightly.

"Shall we unveil Delilah in all her glory, Anisha?" Tom asks.

"Let's do it together," I say. So, Tom, Cleo and I all grab corners of the sheet that is covering the statue. We count to three – **One! Two! Three!** – and pull the sheet off.

Delilah looks **amazing!** The staff have decorated her base with flowers and twinkling lights. Her mended wing looks so good. And where the yellow paint splodges were on her body, they've stuck more patches of colourful fabric so now Delilah is an explosion of colours and patterns all over.

As we're all admiring Delilah, an older man comes along. Tom smiles and says, "Ah, Anisha,

I want to introduce you and your family to someone. This is my grandfather, Jacob. Grandad, this is Anisha, the girl I told you about this morning."

Jacob shakes my hand. "I've heard extraordinary things about you, Anisha. I want to say thank you very much for saving our celebration and our Delilah."

"You're very welcome," I say. "I just couldn't stand by and watch Cleo take the blame for something she didn't do."

"I'll let you into a secret," Jacob says. "I was a bit of a prankster when I was a boy – nothing as big as this, of course, but I got my fair share of telling-offs.

Anyway, those three have said they're sorry and they're going to be making amends for what they did by cleaning up duck poo down by the river for the rest of the season." He chuckles. "It's a real pain to get off the park paths!"

"Ducks poo every fifteen minutes, you know," Milo tells us all proudly.

"Yes, well that should keep young Rae and her friends busy then," says Jacob.

The party for the park's anniversary is **incredible**. There's so much yummy food, which keeps Milo and Manny busy of course. Aunty Bindi has as usual made lots of friends and she drags Uncle Tony over to meet everyone. Then, from nowhere, she pulls out her painting of him from the class they did. Her friends all pull out their paintings too and Uncle Tony is suddenly faced with ten different versions of himself. He laughs and says how good they all are.

There's a dance floor with a DJ playing music. All of us get up and have a little dance – **even me!**

Well, I stay on the edge of the dance floor, but that still counts, right? Milo and Manny do forward rolls and jump up and down, while Mindy bops about in her chair, still being careful of that ankle. Even Mum and Dad have a go. Dad's got some moves – has he been watching YouTube videos with Manny again?

The entertainment team have set up an archery board at the far end of the party, facing away from the guests and under the supervision of the instructor. Granny shows off her archery skills. She shoots an arrow at a melon and it splits into four pieces! She really is very good!

I see Mr Judge in the crowd and he gives me a nod. I do an awkward wave back.

princess_bindirella

princess_bindirella

Dillon comes over, smiling. "How are you, number one mystery solver?" He smiles.

"We couldn't have done it without you!" I say.

"Thank you, it was fun working together. I don't make friends on holidays usually, but I liked hanging out with you guys," Dillon admits. "And guess what? I just found out that my video, well, *our* video of last night **won Prankfest!** Five hundred pounds! It didn't feel right to keep it and my parents suggested we could do something good with it so I wanted to ask you what you thought about donating it to a conservation charity that helps forest wildlife in the area."

"That's **amazing**, Dillon – although I'm not sure I want to encourage your pranking..."
I say.

"I wouldn't mind seeing the video though."

Dillon cackles. "I thought you'd never ask."

He pulls out his phone and we watch the video. With Manny's quacking and the look on Rae's, Jamil's and Bobby's faces when they think Delilah is talking to them, I have to admit it is quite funny.

We watch it twice before Manny, Mindy and Milo come and drag Dillon away to get ice cream with them. I stay where I am, sitting down on the grass and just taking in the scene of the party. I like watching people and the quirky things they do. It's one of my favourite things to do – after reading, of course.

Reading. I never did get to read my big pile of books. Maybe once I'm home I can catch up. We were supposed to go to the reading nook and never got the chance...

Cleo comes and sits next to me. "We never got to have our hot chocolate and chill in the reading nook," she says.

"I was just thinking that!" I say.

"Well, you've got to come back for that free weekend visit that Tom gave you, so maybe we can do it then." Cleo smiles. "Tom just offered me more holiday work, so when I'm not studying or at space camp I'll be here."

"That's great!" I say. "I'm so glad things worked out."

"Only because of you, my friend. Only because of you," Cleo says. "Thank you, Anisha. You will stay in touch, won't you?"

"Definitely," I say.

"Good, because my mum wants you to come for dinner in a few weeks," laughs Cleo.

We hug goodbye and Cleo goes off to help out with the rest of the celebrations.

"This has been a great trip, hasn't it, Anni?" Mum asks as she sits down and puts her arm round me.

"It has – but can I ask one little thing for our next holiday?" I say.

"Of course, **beta**, what is it? You'd prefer the beach next time?"

"Oh, I don't mind where we go. It's just can we not accidentally walk into the middle of a crime or sabotage or vandalism next time?" I laugh.

Mum laughs too. "Hmm… Well, I'm sorry, **beta**, but I think that might be your talent – walking into places where your **super** mystery-solving skills are most needed."

A little while later, as the party dies down, Dad rounds everyone up. "We'd better hit the road soon, family, we don't want to get back home too late. The car's packed up already."

"OHHHHH," everyone groans. "Do we have to go now?"

Dad looks around. "Well, what else do you want to do?" he asks.

"One last activity?" Granny grins.

"Like what?" asks Aunty Bindi.

"Well, I tried this great thing the other day," Granny starts. "Anisha and I already did it, and it was the most **thrilling, amazing** time I've had in ages. You'd love it. In fact, I think we should all do it together."

"You don't mean…?" I start to say.

Granny winks at me. "Let's go, everyone, you're going to love it!"

"Sounds fun," says Dad.

Everyone starts to follow Granny Jas as I shout, **"NOOOOOOOOOOO!"**

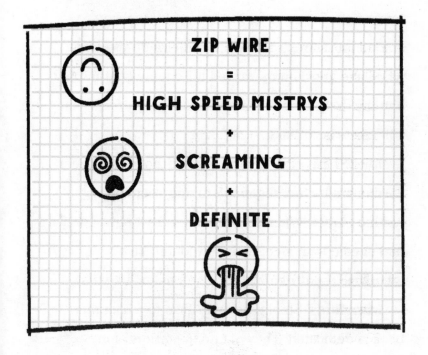

ZIP WIRE

=

HIGH SPEED MISTRYS

+

SCREAMING

+

DEFINITE

ACKNOWLEDGEMENTS

Every time I come round to this part, I feel very emotional. There is a huge team behind this series who have loved and nurtured it from the beginning and my gratitude to them for making my dreams come true is endless.

Kate Shaw, my amazing agent, who brings cheer, wisdom and a firm foot forward approach to my writing career. When I first met her, I thought I only had one book in me. She believed and knew otherwise. I don't know how, she's magic like that.

My editors, Stephanie and Alice, to whom this book is dedicated. They are jump-starters of my stories when they stall and a steady hand to keep me on track. They are lots of laughter, embracers of my silly ideas and givers of the most thoughtful feedback, all of which make me feel like I can do this. Even when I think I can't.

Emma McCann who amazes me every time with her wonderful, hilarious illustrations. Thank you for bringing my characters to life. I hope we get to work together for many more books.

Kat, Stevie, Jess, Sarah, Will and everyone at Usborne. Team Anisha is still the most joyous, supportive and amazing team I could ever ask to be part of. Thank you.

To everyone who supports this series and me. Author friends, near and far, readers, teachers, librarians, bloggers and booksellers. I hope you enjoyed this story and thank you so much for continuing to pick up my books.

Finally, all my love to my family who inspire me every day even if they don't mean to. I'm sorry if something you said or did ends up in a book one day. It's kind of your own fault for being so funny and awesome.

MEET THE AUTHOR

Name: Serena Kumari Patel

Lives with: My brilliant family, Deepak, Alyssa and Reiss

Favourite Subjects: Science and History

Ambitions: To learn to ride a bike (I never learned as a kid).

To keep trying things I'm scared of.

To write lots more books.

Most embarrassing moment:

Singing in Hindi at a talent show and getting most of the words wrong. I hid in the loo after!